A Death at Rosings

by

Renata McMann

&

Summer Hanford

By Renata McMann and Summer Hanford
The Second Mrs. Darcy
Georgiana's Folly (The Wickham Coin Book 1)
Elizabeth's Plight (The Wickham Coin Book 2)
The above two books have been published in a single volume as:
Georgiana's Folly & Elizabeth's Plight: Wickham Coin Series,
volumes 1 & 2
Caroline and the Footman
The Scandalous Stepmother
Mr. Collins' Deception
Poor Mr. Darcy
Mary Younge

With special thanks to our editor, Joanne Girard
Cover by Summer Hanford

Other *Pride and Prejudice* variations by Renata McMann
Heiress to Longbourn
Pemberley Weddings
The Inconsistency of Caroline Bingley
Three Daughters Married
Anne de Bourgh Manages
The above works are collected in the book: *Five Pride and Prejudice Variations*

Also by Renata McMann
Journey Towards a Preordained Time

Books by Renata McMann writing as Teresa McCullough

Enhancer Novels
These are all stand-alone novels in the same universe
Enhancers Campaign
The First Enhancer
The Pirates of Fainting Goat Island
The Enhancer with Meg Baxter

Bengt/Tian stories
The Secret of Sanctua A Bengt/Tian novel
Kidnapped by Fae: a Bengt/Tian Short Story

Other stories
The Slave of Duty with Meg Baxter
Lost Past

Also by Summer Hanford

Short Stories by Summer Hanford
The Forging of Cadwel
Hawk Trials for Mirimel
The Fall of Larkesong
The Sword of Three

Novels by Summer Hanford
Gift of the Aluien
Hawks of Sorga
Throne of Wheylia
Coming in 2016
The Plains of Tybrunn

Contents

Chapter One

As Elizabeth walked the half mile to Rosings, she was glad Mr. Darcy and his cousin Colonel Fitzwilliam were no longer there, even though Rosings would be less interesting without the two gentlemen. Certainly, her present company would not be entertaining. The absurdities of her cousin Mr. Collins were too predictable. Her good friend Charlotte Collins would defer to their hostess, Lady Catherine. Charlotte's sister Maria Lucas would say little because she had little to say. Lady Catherine's daughter and her daughter's companion would say almost nothing. Lady Catherine would do most of the talking with Mr. Collins supporting her and praising her.

Elizabeth could no longer flirt with Colonel Fitzwilliam or spar with Mr. Darcy. Now that she realized she'd been wrong about Mr. Darcy, she also realized she found her verbal battles with him stimulating. This evening at Rosings would offer neither the pleasure of Colonel Fitzwilliam nor the challenge of Mr. Darcy.

Which brought her to the crux of her ill temper, and to the one thing she was trying chiefly not to think about, Mr. Darcy. Elizabeth frowned, her hands clenching. It irked and embarrassed her that she had so fully misjudged the man. Nearly all of the things she once held against him had been explained away in his lengthy letter, leaving behind a bitter tasting truth: Elizabeth had been completely taken in by Mr. Wickham.

She was ashamed she'd ignored the evidence of the inconsistencies of Wickham's actions and believed his lies. He'd made a fool of her, and she let him. All because Mr. Darcy had pricked her pride, saying she wasn't handsome enough to dance with. What a silly, shallow creature she turned out to be. She smiled wryly. She would never have guessed it of herself.

Darcy's letter even explained why he'd warned Mr. Bingley off her sister Jane. Elizabeth could understand his reasoning. She could even grudgingly admit that Jane was often hard to fathom, for it was difficult to know where her kind nature left off and her true feelings began. Mr. Darcy had been wrong to come between them, though. Of that, at least, Elizabeth was still confident. He'd ruined Jane's happiness and Elizabeth couldn't forgive him for that. She pulled that thought about her, using it as a balm for her bad judgment in refusing Darcy's proposal with such animosity.

Nor should she forgive him for the nature of that proposal. Elizabeth hadn't thought anyone could deliver a less flattering offer than her cousin had put to her, but Mr. Darcy's request made Mr. Collins' proposal sound like one of Shakespeare's sonnets of love. Great men like Mr. Darcy, she supposed, must do everything in a magnificent fashion, even be it insulting Elizabeth and all those she loved.

Still, as angry as his proposal made her, she wished she hadn't misjudged him. Not that the content of his letter would have influenced her answer. Even a more charming proposal wouldn't have. All the money in England couldn't persuade her to marry where she held no regard.

She and her companions reached Rosings, the door opening before they could knock, and she resolved to set aside her inner disquiet. Elizabeth was not formed for ill humor. She intended to enjoy herself in spite of the circumstances.

They were shown into the ostentatious parlor Lady Catherine preferred, where their hostess awaited them. After greetings were exchanged, Mr. Collins perched on the edge of the chair adjacent to Lady Catherine, fixing his reverent gaze on her. "May I say your ladyship is looking in fine health this evening."

"You may not," Lady Catherine said. "I feel abysmal."

That certainly stopped the conversation.

Elizabeth sat next to the frail heiress Miss de Bourgh, who nodded slightly in greeting. Miss de Bourgh hadn't spoken a word yet, having relied on her mother to make her greetings for her. Elizabeth couldn't help wondering, should Mr. Darcy ever marry his cousin as Lady Catherine wished, if the two would ever speak. Miss de Bourgh seemed even more reluctant to do so than he was.

"One wouldn't suspect you aren't feeling yourself by looking at you. You look quite well, my lady," Charlotte said, earning her a smile from Mr. Collins.

"Well, I'm not," Lady Catherine snapped. "I should know how I feel far better than any of you."

Elizabeth privately agreed with the lady's assessment of herself. Lady Catherine looked grayer than usual and her shoulders slumped under the weight of her thick fur tippet.

"Is there anything I can get for you?" Mr. Collins asked. "Shall I send a servant for anything?"

"I am perfectly capable of requesting whatever I like from my own servants," Lady Catherine said.

"Of course, of course," Mr. Collins said, looking about helplessly.

Lady Catherine's temper was even shorter than usual, Elizabeth reflected, or perhaps she was more acutely aware of the lady's temperament than normal, given recent occurrences. Elizabeth could not see Lady Catherine without recollecting that, had she chosen it, she might by this time have been presented to her as her future niece; nor could she think, without a smile, of what her ladyship's indignation would have been. "What would she have said? How would she have behaved?" were questions with which she amused herself.

Silence fell again and Elizabeth struggled to set aside her musings and think of something suitable to say. She wished for more guests to provide conversation, though she could understand why the local families were reluctant to augment the guest list. Though excellent, Lady Catherine's cook simply wasn't talented enough to draw people in at the price of listening to her ladyship all evening, though Elizabeth didn't know if there was a cook alive who would be.

Really though, with Mr. and Mrs. Collins, Maria, Miss de Bourgh, Mrs. Jenkinson and herself in the room, there ought to be enough for one conversation to take place, if not two ongoing. Usually, Lady Catherine did all of the speaking, using them as an audience for her close-minded notions and ideas. Elizabeth scrutinized her more closely, wondering how unwell Lady Catherine felt. It wasn't like her to remain silent before so many guests.

Lady Catherine just sat, her mouth clamped tightly shut and gray about the edges. Elizabeth glanced at Charlotte, wondering if they should send for a doctor and if she dared suggest as much. If Lady Catherine wasn't as ill as she looked, the question would only aggravate her.

"Mother," Miss de Bourgh cried.

Elizabeth swiveled back around to watch Lady Catherine topple sideways on the settee, her eyes open wide in shock. Mrs. Jenkinson ran across the room, dropping to her knees before Lady Catherine. Mr. Collins sat with a startled look on his face, his hands gripping the arms of his chair, but Charlotte jumped up. It took Elizabeth a moment to realize she was standing as well.

"Mr. Collins, Lady Catherine is ill. Get a doctor," Elizabeth ordered in an urgent voice.

Mr. Collins turned to look at her, his mouth hanging open.

"She's right," Charlotte said, crossing to stand between him and their hostess. "You're the best one to send for a doctor. Hurry."

"Yes, yes of course," he mumbled, coming unsteadily to his feet.

He stumbled from the room, glancing back at nearly every step. Elizabeth moved back out of his way. She would have told him to hurry, but from what she could see from where she stood, there was likely little to be done for Lady Catherine.

"Maria, see to Miss de Bourgh," Charlotte ordered her sister as she knelt by Mrs. Jenkinson's side. "Lady Catherine seems to be struggling to breath. Hand me those pillows, Elizabeth. Let's loosen her collar," she added to Mrs. Jenkinson.

Elizabeth gathered the pillows and helped Charlotte and Mrs. Jenkinson prop up their ashen and gasping hostess. She stepped back again while Charlotte unwound the tippet and unfastened the buttons at Lady Catherine's neck. A glance in their direction showed her that Maria had pulled her chair closer to Miss de Bourgh's and held her hands, though it was difficult to say which of the two looked more frightened.

"Elizabeth, could you send for Lady Catherine's maid, please?"

Elizabeth nodded and went to the door. She was glad Charlotte was taking charge, knowing her to be a capable and leveled headed person. Turning to the nervous looking footman standing without, Elizabeth said, "Could you please ask Lady Catherine's maid to come immediately?"

"Yes, miss," the man said, hurrying away.

"Do you think we should remove her to her room?" Mrs. Jenkinson said as Elizabeth turned from the doorway.

"I think we should wait for the doctor to decide," Charlotte said. "She seems better able to breath now." She peered down at a diminished looking Lady Catherine. "My lady, can you hear me? It's Mrs. Collins. Can you tell us what's wrong? What do you need?"

Lady Catherine looked up at Charlotte with glazed eyes. Her lips moved slightly, but the only sound to come out was a low, meaningless mumble. Miss de Bourgh choked back a sob, pulling her hands from Maria's to cover her face. Charlotte looked over her shoulder at Elizabeth, nodding in Miss de Bourgh's direction in a meaningful way.

"Miss de Bourgh," Elizabeth said, crossing the room to stand before her chair. "May I send for your maid? Would you like me to assist you to your room?"

Miss de Bourgh nodded. She struggled to her feet, dropping her hands to reveal a pallid, tear-streaked face. For the first time, the enormity of what was happening struck Elizabeth. Lady Catherine might very well be dying, leaving Miss de Bourgh with no mother, siblings or father. Only more distant relatives would remain.

Impulsively, Elizabeth embraced Miss de Bourgh. Though some of them might vex Elizabeth at times, she couldn't imagine a world with no parents or sisters in it. Miss de Bourgh went ridged for a moment before dropping her head to Elizabeth's shoulder, muted sobs shaking her thin frame. Behind her, Elizabeth could hear Charlotte trying to rouse Lady Catherine in gentle tones.

Elizabeth held Miss de Bourgh, offering what comfort she could. When she stepped back, Maria pressed a kerchief into her hand. Miss de Bourgh blotted her face.

"Thank you," she said, clutching the small handkerchief. "I should like to go to my room now." She looked toward her mother, who still hadn't spoken.

Elizabeth nodded, taking Miss de Bourgh's arm and helping her across the room, Maria trailing behind them. Elizabeth's last glance at Lady Catherine showed her color to be unimproved and her eyes closed. They passed her crying maid coming down the hallway as they walked slowly toward the stairs.

Chapter Two

Elizabeth woke quickly the next morning as the events of the evening before crowded into her thoughts. She sat up, wondering if there was any news of Lady Catherine, for she and Maria had returned to the parsonage before the doctor had arrived. After settling Miss de Bourgh into her room with her maid and waiting for some time to see if she could be useful, Elizabeth had decided the best they could do was to stay out of people's way. She bid Charlotte goodnight and took Maria Lucas with her.

They had only just turned off the drive when a carriage had come racing up at a dangerous speed. Elizabeth assumed the carriage held the doctor. Perhaps, she mused as she made quick work of readying for the day, running people down was one of the ways the man created new patients.

She let that notion entertain her as she made her way to the parlor to find Charlotte already there. She looked tired, the skin around her eyes puffy and her face pale. Elizabeth wondered how late she'd stayed up and why she was already out of bed.

"I'm surprised to see you up so early," she said, sitting down across from Charlotte.

"Up early?" Charlotte said. She turned blurry eyes to Elizabeth. "I haven't yet gone to bed."

"Then you're silly," Elizabeth said. "Why ever don't you go now? When did you return?"

"Only a short time ago. I thought I would wait for Mr. Collins. He's still at Rosings, trying to help Miss de Bourgh with arrangements for the funeral."

"Lady Catherine died?" Elizabeth asked, shocked. She hadn't

realized. No wonder Charlotte and Mr. Collins had stayed the entire night. "When? What did the doctor say?"

"He said it was her heart," Charlotte said. She rubbed at her already red eyes. "It happened a few hours ago. Miss de Bourgh is very distraught, as is the staff. No one knows what to do."

"Surly family will be sent for?" Elizabeth said, wondering if that meant Mr. Darcy would return.

"Yes, Mr. Collins has been helping Miss de Bourgh dispatch letters."

"I would think Miss de Bourgh would be capable of writing her relatives without his help. Is she truly that distressed?" Elizabeth also thought Miss de Bourgh, or most anyone, would prefer writing their letters without Mr. Collins hovering nearby.

"He's doing all he can to ingratiate himself." Charlotte's tone was touched with annoyance. She sighed, rubbing her eyes again. "He doesn't seem to realize that he'll hold the living regardless of who owns Rosings. There's no reason for him to toady to Miss de Bourgh, any more than there was for his continued adoration of Lady Catherine. I think it must be his nature to behave so."

"So Miss de Bourgh is to inherit, then?"

"Everyone seems to believe so, but I don't think it's been made certain."

Elizabeth nodded. She thought of the frail, closeted heiress and the trouble that was sure to come her way. "Well, she won't be shy of suitors," Elizabeth said dryly. "I can't imagine her coping with all that she needs to do." Writing letters was one thing, but managing Rosings and fending off opportunistic men was another. If Elizabeth had been so easily taken in by a man like Mr. Wickham, what chance did someone as completely inexperienced as Miss de Bourgh have of seeing through similar gentlemen?

"Mr. Collins and I will do what we can, and family is being sent for," Charlotte reiterated. "There's nothing more to be done. We must hope that, when she weds, she chooses well, for her sake and ours. Mr. Collins will likely spend a great deal of time with whomever Miss de

Bourgh takes to husband."

Elizabeth wasn't sure of that. She couldn't imagine most people wishing to be so much in Mr. Collins' company as Lady Catherine had. "Would your life be easier if Miss de Bourgh chose to distance herself from him?"

"I don't know," Charlotte said. "Perhaps Mr. Collins would spend more of his time attending to his parishioners, or perhaps he would devote himself to winning Miss de Bourgh's and her husband's favor. I'm not sure if either would alter my life significantly. Hopefully, she'll seek advice and we can influence her into a good match."

Elizabeth nodded, but she wasn't sure she approved. She could understand Charlotte's desire to have an amiable patron, but if Charlotte and Mr. Collins were giving advice crafted with their best interests in mind, would that advice also be what was best for Miss de Bourgh? There was a time when Elizabeth would have assured anyone that Charlotte was the soul of integrity and could be trusted to give Miss de Bourgh advice completely lacking in selfishness, but that time was past.

She knew the moment of its passing, and it saddened her. She remembered what she'd told Jane when they'd discussed Charlotte's acceptance of Mr. Collins' proposal. Jane, as was her nature, had defended Charlotte. Elizabeth had replied, "You shall not, for the sake of one individual, change the meaning of principle and integrity." Charlotte had married solely for financial reasons. Elizabeth didn't know if she'd ever be able to forgive her.

"I should see to some tea for us, if you're insistent on waiting up," Elizabeth said, standing abruptly. She needed something to distract her from her uncharitable thoughts. Charlotte was her friend.

"Thank you," Charlotte said, resting her chin in her hands. "You must wish for breakfast, as well. I doubt the servants are sure what to do, as we were gone all night."

"I'll let them know," Elizabeth said. She crossed to the door.

"I hope Mr. Darcy doesn't marry her," Charlotte mused, her voice soft. "I can't imagine life with him looming over us, so severe all of the time."

Elizabeth headed down the hall, searching for a maid. She had no notion of Mr. Darcy's intentions toward Miss de Bourgh, but he was the one man she trusted not to marry her for money. Firstly, because he was reputed to be wealthy in his own right. Secondly and more significantly, because of his proposal to her.

In spite of how belittling his proposal had been, he'd obviously meant to marry her for love. He couldn't help but be aware that she brought no financial gain to a union. In truth, a man as intelligent as Mr. Darcy would surely realize Elizabeth was likely to cost him money. As her husband, he would be required to support her mother when her father died, and any of her unmarried sisters. When looked at through such heavy obligations, Elizabeth supposed it was quite flattering that he'd proposed.

Even if she hadn't such irrefutable evidence that Mr. Darcy wasn't inclined to marry for fortune, his letter had revealed a man of integrity. If Mr. Darcy gave Miss de Bourgh advice, it would be sound advice not marked by his own interests. Hopefully, for Miss de Bourgh's sake, he was one of the relatives summoned soonest.

"Can I help you, miss?" a voice asked.

Elizabeth realized she was standing outside the kitchen, lost in thought.

"Mrs. Collins would like some tea," she said.

"Yes, miss," the woman replied, dropping a curtsy.

"I'm pleased to help," Elizabeth said.

"That won't be necessary, miss," the maid answered as she turned away. She entered the kitchen, swinging the door closed behind her.

Elizabeth smiled slightly. She knew Charlotte helped in the kitchen, but she'd little notion of what would be helpful. She wondered if the maid was keeping her out because she was a guest, or if Charlotte had warned her staff that Elizabeth was useless for such tasks.

How to be valuable in the kitchen was likely something she'd have to learn now that she had passed up two suitors, Elizabeth reflected. She headed back toward the parlor, an image of Mr. Darcy's face as she'd last seen him, when he'd handed her the letter, filling her mind. Though she'd badly misjudged the man, she was still sure she'd done the right thing in refusing him. She was, however, sorry she'd done so with quite so much acrimony.

She returned to the parlor to find Mr. Collins coming out, looking even more exhausted than Charlotte. "Cousin Elizabeth," he called, hurrying toward her. "You must make haste to Rosings. Miss de Bourgh wishes your presence there."

"I haven't yet had breakfast," Elizabeth protested. She was growing rather hungry, having made do with a light meal hastily put together by Charlotte's cook the previous evening.

"That doesn't matter," he said. He wrung his hands. "She's asking for you. She was quite insistent."

"What does she want me for?" Elizabeth asked, dubious that it was actually anything important.

"I didn't presume to inquire," he said. "Come. We must hurry."

He took her arm, ushering her outside. There was no carriage, of course. Elizabeth wondered if Miss de Bourgh agreed with her mother's policy of conveying people away from Rosings but not to it, or if no one in her household had the presence of mind to send one. Mr. Collins set a quick pace, but Elizabeth kept up with ease.

"We really must hurry," he repeated. "Oh, that my patroness, Lady Catherine, should die, and with Miss de Bourgh still unwed. What a terrible thing. Hardly a worse thing could have happened. We have to hurry."

Elizabeth broke into a run. Mr. Collins' exhausted ramblings were not to be endured. He wished her to hurry, so she would, right away from him. She smiled, pleased with both the exertion and the solution. It felt wonderful to be making all haste across the yard, the wind blowing through her hair and catching her clothing as she ran.

She slowed to a walk before reaching the door, so as not to be breathless when she entered, especially as there was likely no real reason for haste. What, after all, could possibly be so urgent? Elizabeth had no special skills that Miss de Bourgh could be in need of.

Somewhat to her surprise, she was immediately shown into Miss de Bourgh's presence, though she wasn't taken to the parlor where Lady Catherine had habitually received guests. The room Miss de Bourgh awaited her in was no less richly appointed, but more understated. Elizabeth preferred it immensely to the other, more ornate, parlor. Looking around, Elizabeth realized the heiress was alone and wondered where Mrs. Jenkinson was. "Miss de Bourgh," she greeted, curtsying. "May I express my condolences on your loss?"

"Thank you," Miss de Bourgh said. She was seated on a settee, a shawl clenched about her shoulders and a blanket in her lap like a woman three times her age. She looked pale, and her eyes were slightly red from crying, but she didn't look as if she'd cried recently. "I assume Mr. Collins sent you?"

"He accompanied me, but I was a bit faster," Elizabeth said.

"Could you please advise the footman outside that I don't wish our conversation to be disturbed, then, and close the door? I want to speak to you in private."

"Of course," Elizabeth said, realizing that must be why Mrs. Jenkinson was absent. She returned to the doorway. "Miss de Bourgh asks that we remain undisturbed." The footman nodded and Elizabeth slid the door shut.

"You must be wondering why I asked to see you," Miss de Bourgh said as Elizabeth returned. "Please, sit down." She gestured to the sofa opposite her.

"I am curious, but assume you will tell me," Elizabeth said. She seated herself in the indicated spot. A low table stood between them and she wondered if Miss de Bourgh would offer refreshments.

"It's a little hard to explain," Miss de Bourgh said. Her eyes took on a distant look.

Elizabeth suppressed a sigh. She supposed it was too much to ask

18

that someone would think of her stomach when Lady Catherine had so recently died.

"As I suppose you can imagine, I had a sickly childhood," Miss de Bourgh continued. "I caught everything that went around. The doctor said that if someone had a cold in the next village, I would catch it. I was kept home and barely educated. I now realize it wouldn't have hurt me to learn while I had a cold, but that apparently never occurred to anyone at the time. I had four brothers who all died of various illnesses and my father was frantic in protecting me. I thought when he died four years ago that I would have more freedom, but I've had less."

"That must have been very difficult," Elizabeth said with automatic sympathy. Whatever complaints she had about her parents' skills at being parents, they were not overly protective. Not even of Kitty, who was a bit frail, or of Lydia, who was more than a bit silly.

"It was," Miss de Bourgh said. "Losing my brothers was difficult, although I scarcely recall them. Losing my father was harder. That was even worse than having no freedom, because he was the one person who truly cared how I felt. My mother always seemed to look on me as some sort of dissatisfying personal accessory."

"I'm sure that's not true," Elizabeth protested. "She protected you because she cared for you."

Miss de Bourgh shrugged. "Perhaps. I suppose there's no way to discover the truth of that now." She shut her eyes for a moment. Whether in grief or from fatigue, Elizabeth didn't know.

"Eventually, I realized I could learn about the world from books," Miss de Bourgh said. "I began to sneak them from our library. I employed the same aspect of myself that my mother used to control me, my health. I convinced Mrs. Jenkinson that I need a long nap each afternoon, and extra sleep at night. I cultivated the notion that I require candles burning by my bedside for comfort. During all the extra time I'm allowed to myself, unsupervised, I read."

"What do you read?" Elizabeth asked, intrigued. There was more to Miss de Bourgh than she'd expected. In fact, Miss de Bourgh had hid

19

that she had any mind at all so well, Elizabeth had been completely fooled. She smiled to herself. If this sort of thing kept up, she would be forced to conclude that she was an abysmal judge of character.

"Everything in our library."

"Your library looks like it has a lot of books." An impressive number to collect, Elizabeth thought, and an even more impressive number to read. She made no pretense of having read all of the books in her father's library, and it was nowhere near the size of the one at Rosings.

"There are five hundred and seventy-three. Yes, I counted them once. I've read them all. Some, I've read two or three times. I've read about philosophy, law and agriculture. I've read sermons and poetry. I've read *Gulliver's Travels* and *Moll Flanders*. I've read *A Vindication of the Rights of Woman* by Mary Wollstonecraft. Even when I've read a book before, I sometimes stay up late rereading it. When I wake up looking tired, everyone assumes I'm ill."

"Have you read much that was published recently?" Elizabeth asked. She'd seen the library only once, but recalled many of the books looked quite old, as if the masters of Rosings had ceased adding to their collection at some point in the past. While all information was good, some topics changed enough over time to benefit from a more modern approach.

"I've bribed a couple of servants to bring me newspapers. I've arranged with one of the tenants to order books. I read them, and either hide them in a trunk I keep locked or give them to her to sell. Fortunately, no one pays much attention to my pocket money, since it comes from the interest on my dowry and is very generous."

"If you inherit Rosings, you won't have to read in secret. You'll be able to add your books to Rosings' collection."

"My assumption is that I will only inherit Rosings in a way, but it will be enough of a way. My mother had life interest in Rosings, as will I. Though I won't be able to sell it, and don't wish to, I will have everything of the running of the estate and the benefits of it. That income is more than ample for my foreseeable needs. My mother also had a personal fortune. I believe it to be about forty thousand pounds. I'll probably inherit most of it, though I tried to talk her into willing my cousin Richard something significant. He and Darcy help with the estate. Richard deserves something for so many years of care."

"Richard?" Elizabeth asked, unsure who she meant, though she guessed that must be Colonel Fitzwilliam's given name.

"Colonel Fitzwilliam," Miss de Bourgh confirmed. "I didn't ask Mother to do anything for Darcy. He has plenty of money of his own."

If Miss de Bourgh knew of Darcy's offer to her, would she have had the tact not to mention the fortune Elizabeth had turned down? More likely, if Miss de Bourgh knew of Darcy's offer they wouldn't be having the conversation at all. "That seems logical. Colonel Fitzwilliam seems a worthy man on whom to bestow a windfall. I still don't understand why you're telling me all of this, though."

"I know books. I don't know people. I don't know life. In recent years, we rarely even had guests. Not even the neighbors. It will likely come as no shock to you that many of them didn't like my mother. Most claimed to be too busy to visit. Some may have been willing to come back, but she didn't like them, especially anyone who was provoked to impoliteness by her impertinent questions."

"Mr. and Mrs. Collins always seem happy to visit, and Mr. Darcy and Colonel Fitzwilliam were only recently here," Elizabeth protested, not wanting Miss de Bourgh to feel too much alone in the world.

"Mr. and Mrs. Collins were always good enough to put up with Mother," Miss de Bourgh said. "I think he may even have genuinely enjoyed her attention, though I find the idea hard to believe. As for Darcy and Richard, they visited out of familial obligation. They made their time here go smoothly by always giving in to Mother."

"I can think of one point on which Mr. Darcy didn't seem ready to give in to your mother," Elizabeth couldn't resist making the reference. She found she wanted to know where Miss de Bourgh's thoughts were on the issue of her near engagement to Mr. Darcy.

"Yes, on the issue of his marrying me." Miss de Bourgh's eyes narrowed. "You should know, I think, that I never wanted to marry Darcy. Mother wouldn't believe me, of course, but she never listened to anything I said. She didn't think I had a mind. I wouldn't want you to ever feel that I had any intentions toward Darcy."

Elizabeth felt her face heat slightly and wished she hadn't allowed her curiosity to direct the conversation to so delicate a subject. "I still don't know why you wished to talk with me," she said, changing the subject. Perhaps Miss de Bourgh simply wanted to talk to someone? She didn't have any friends. Not that Elizabeth knew of, at any rate. "Wouldn't Mrs. Jenkinson be a better person to talk to about all of this?"

"Absolutely not," Miss de Bourgh said in a firm tone. "She never wishes to speak to me about anything other than my health. Anything I do say to her, she used to report back to my mother. I haven't told her yet, but I'm letting her go."

"Does she have a place to go?" Elizabeth asked, shocked. Mrs. Jenkinson likely thought her position quite secure. Normally it would be, but Elizabeth agreed that Miss de Bourgh shouldn't gloss over years of spying. She wondered why Miss de Bourgh hadn't replaced her companion with someone more trustworthy long ago.

"I don't care if she has a place to go," Miss de Bourgh said.

Elizabeth raised her eyebrows.

"Yes, I do care," Miss de Bourgh amended with a sigh. "I'll be arranging a pension for her. It will be through the bank, since I don't want to be bothered. She has five siblings and numerous nephews and nieces. I'm sure one of them will be glad to have her and her pension, although it will be enough for her to live alone if she chooses."

"That's very generous of you," Elizabeth said, still confused. If Miss de Bourgh cared enough to be so generous, why was she letting the woman go? It wasn't as if she could still spy for Lady Catherine. Elizabeth supposed the bond of trust was irreparably broken. An unhappy suspicion built in her. If Miss de Bourgh was letting Mrs. Jenkinson go . . . "Why do you want me?"

"I want you to be my companion."

"Your companion? I can't do that!" Elizabeth was not quite insulted. It was actually a good offer for someone who had as little chance of finding marital happiness as she seemed to. She wasn't willing to give up on her own household yet, though, and forever label herself a spinster and ladies' companion. Why, she may as well become a governess and work for a living.

"No, of course not. You are neither married nor a widow," Miss de Bourgh said. "I chose my words poorly. I asked a distant cousin to come. She will fill that role. Mrs. Allen. She's biddable and won't interfere with my life. All she wants is a good table."

Elizabeth relaxed slightly. "What do you mean, then, by companion?"

"I need a friend. Someone I can ask guidance from. As I said, I don't know anything yet about interacting in the real world, only in books. My uncle, my mother's brother, is sure to try to impose someone on me. He'll ignore that I have Mrs. Allen here for the same reason I want her; she won't control me."

"Surly Mr. Darcy and Colonel Fitzwilliam will offer you guidance? Your uncle can't fail to be pleased with that."

Miss de Bourgh nodded. "I agree, they are certain to advise me, and I shall consider any advice they give. Their advice will assuredly be in keeping with what they see as my best interests. I wonder, though, if it will always be in keeping with my wishes? I want someone I can trust to be on my side." She looked at Elizabeth with pleading eyes. "I need someone who places me first, Miss Bennet. Above Rosings."

What Miss de Bourgh needed was a loving husband, but Elizabeth didn't know how to produce one of those. She and her four unmarried sisters were proof enough of her inability to do so. She pressed her lips together, trying to think of a polite way to refuse what was a rather daunting offer.

"I don't want another man telling me what to do," Miss de Bourgh said, almost as if she could read Elizabeth's thoughts. "I'll have enough of that with Darcy, Colonel Fitzwilliam and my uncle. I want a woman's point of view, and I need someone who can stand up to them, or they'll run Rosings and I'll sit alone and useless in this giant house, day in and day out, until my entire life has passed me by."

Elizabeth could sympathize, but Miss de Bourgh was asking too much of her, especially if she was supposed to stand up to Mr. Darcy, whom she hardly wished to see again, let alone argue with. She didn't care to add any more insult there, earned or erroneous. "I have a home," she said. "My father misses me already."

"I'm not asking you to stay forever," Miss de Bourgh said. "Only until I learn to manage Rosings. I'm not a foolish person. I'm sure I can learn with some rapidity, and I'll have the imminence of your departure to spur me on. Please, Miss Bennet. I really have nowhere else to turn."

"I might stay for a week or two," Elizabeth said, moved. "But no longer. I have a life of my own to live." Even as she said it, she wondered how she was meant to stand up *for* Miss de Bourgh when she couldn't even stand up *to* her. If Miss de Bourgh was aware of the irony of Elizabeth's capitulation, it didn't show on her face.

"Two weeks won't be enough," Miss de Bourgh said. "I know I'm asking a lot and that you should receive some sort of compensation for giving up your time. I'm willing to pay you one hundred pounds a month. If you stay for a year, and invest it, you'll have fifty or sixty pounds a year off it in interest."

Elizabeth shook her head, opening her mouth to decline, although she knew the offer was extraordinarily generous.

"You can leave anytime you like and I'll give you transportation home," Miss de Bourgh continued before Elizabeth could speak. "I'll give you a small amount of spending money as well, while you're here. I know your father's estate is entailed to Mr. Collins. You could buy yourself security with what I'm offering."

"You think you can bribe me to stay?" Elizabeth asked, truly offended this time. Why was it that people who had money assumed that people who didn't have as much would do anything for it? Did they think they were the only ones who could afford integrity?

"I wish I could," Miss de Bourgh, sinking back against the settee. She looked wan, and frail. "I don't believe you to be bribable. I suppose if you were, I wouldn't want your help so desperately. Don't be insulted."

"I most certainly won't be, if you aren't insulting me," Elizabeth said. She took a deep breath, trying to apply logic to the situation. Her father sometimes told her not to be headstrong. In her relationship with Mr. Darcy she'd been headstrong in believing the worst of him and also in insulting him when he proposed. She cringed inwardly, knowing what her father would think of that. Worse, what her mother would. Elizabeth knew she needed to learn to think more of her familial obligations. It wasn't as if Miss de Bourgh was asking her for a lifelong commitment, like Mr. Collins or Mr. Darcy had.

"I'm not insulting you," Miss de Bourgh said. "It isn't a bribe. Believe me, you will earn your money. I know as a gentleman's daughter you aren't used to thinking of earning money, but you can, and without shame. In truth, you'd be almost noble. You can stand between me and my uncle. You can keep me from being an utter fool. I need you. I'm offering money because it is the only currency I know how to deal in."

Miss de Bourgh was giving a better argument than money. Staying a few weeks or even a few months to help someone who needed it was the right thing to do. She could always return home if things became unreasonable. Probably she wouldn't be needed after a month, and that wasn't a lot of time to give someone who seemed to have so much, but in reality had so little.

"Even though I will be in deep mourning, suitors will approach me," Miss de Bourgh said. She leaned forward, looking hopeful, perhaps seeing something of the war waging inside Elizabeth, though she was trying to keep her visage calm. "Maybe you'll catch one. I know from Mrs. Collins that your mother would be upset if you didn't take advantage of that. I'll invite your sisters to visit. They might catch suitors as well."

Elizabeth sighed. No, she couldn't be bribed. Not with money, at least. Love for her family was a different matter, however. Not only that, she realized, looking at the hope on Miss de Bourgh's thin face. Miss de Bourgh truly did need help. Even that morning, Elizabeth had contemplated how few people Miss de Bourgh had in her life, and fewer still whom she could trust. Not that Elizabeth didn't think Mr. Darcy and Colonel Fitzwilliam trustworthy, but did they know their cousin at all? Would they consult Miss de Bourgh and listen to her thoughts, or would they treat her as her mother had and uncle would?

"I'd be honored to stay, Miss de Bourgh," Elizabeth said. "However, I must decline being paid. It doesn't seem right that I should be your guest, sleep under your roof and dine at your table, and also take your money. My conscience won't permit it."

She would content herself with the money her parents would save without her there to feed and with the opportunity to invite her sisters to meet suitors. It was a nice dream, saving up enough to buy security for her sisters, but Elizabeth didn't mean to remain long enough for that dream to ever take shape.

Miss de Bourgh smiled. "I'm so pleased you'll remain," she said. "Are you certain about the money? I really do feel you should be compensated. There's no shame in it."

"I'm adamantly certain," Elizabeth said.

"At least allow me to match whatever amount of pocket money it is you receive from your father," Miss de Bourgh said. "That way, you can allow him to save, or you can have the opportunity to do so."

"That really won't be necessary."

"I insist you either allow me to pay you or take the pocket money," Miss de Bourgh said.

Elizabeth sighed. She was starting to wonder why Miss de Bourgh thought she needed someone to stand up for her. She seemed quite sure of herself. Of course, Elizabeth supposed she was a lot easier to be assertive with than Mr. Darcy or the aforementioned uncle, Lady Catherine's brother. Elizabeth couldn't imagine what a male version of

Lady Catherine would be like. "The pocket money," she said.

"Wonderful. You may move in this afternoon, for I'm sure I'll need you tomorrow. I'll send for the carriage."

"I'll need to write my father for permission to stay away longer," Elizabeth cautioned her, though it was likely a formality.

"Of course, but you can move in while you wait for the return letter, can't you?" Miss de Bourgh asked. "I'll make sure there is stationery in your room."

Elizabeth nodded, standing. She wondered if Miss de Bourgh really needed her in the morning or was worried Elizabeth would change her mind if left to think for longer. "Thank you, Miss de Bourgh."

"Please, call me Anne. Could you ask the footman to step in?"

Elizabeth nodded. "Please call me Elizabeth." She went to the door and slid it open, stepping out to address the footman waiting there. "Miss de Bourgh would like to see you."

The man nodded and went in. Elizabeth could hear Anne telling him to have the carriage made ready and to tell the coachman to take her to the parsonage to collect her belongings. It wasn't until Elizabeth was on her way back later that day, possessions in tow and having eaten a meal at the parsonage, that she realized her capitulation would likely mean she'd be seeing Mr. Darcy again, and soon.

Well, she was supposed to be strong, according to Anne. Although she'd had vague hopes of never having to be in Mr. Darcy's presence again after all that had been said between them, she would have to put those hopes aside in order to meet her commitment to Anne. She'd also have to set aside her anger at his insulting proposal and his interference in Jane's happiness, if she could. It helped that her anger was tempered with her shame over misjudging him so fully. Maybe, she mused as the carriage rolled up Rosings' tree-lined drive, she'd even find the opportunity to apologize to him for that.

She alighted without help when the carriage came to a halt at the foot of Rosings' imposing front entrance. For all she'd amused herself with silently mocking Mr. Collins' awe of the place, it was an impressive manor, and daunting. She hesitated at the bottom step for a moment, wondering if she had any advice for the woman who was to be in charge of such an estate. What, after all, did Elizabeth know about managing a vast holding?

The footman marched past with her belongings and she shook herself, hurrying up the steps. Mr. Darcy and Colonel Fitzwilliam, and likely a dozen other people, would know how to manage Rosings. Elizabeth simply needed to keep Anne from doing anything foolish or being bullied. She could do that. At least, she hoped she could.

Elizabeth entered, finding a maid waiting to show her to her room. Elizabeth hadn't been to the private sections of the manor before, but was unsurprised to find them as opulent as the more public spaces. She looked about the wide hallway she was being led down, wondering if she would ever become accustomed to the almost garish, slightly pretentious decor. She hoped not.

"That's Miss de Bourgh's room," the maid said as they slowed, pointing to the room after the one they stopped at. She opened the door to the room Elizabeth would use, stepping back. "And this will be your room, miss."

"Thank you," Elizabeth said.

"Will you need anything else, miss? Shall I assist you in unpacking?"

"No, thank you," she said.

"Dinner is served in five hours, miss."

Elizabeth nodded, stepping inside and closing the door.

She walked slowly about the room, pleasantly surprised. Not by the richness of it, which far exceeded any room she'd ever slept in, but by the subtlety. Though the furnishings were no less expensive, the bedding she ran her hand along no less luxurious, than anything else she'd encountered in Rosings, it was all much more understated. From the gentle curves of the writing desk to the subtle embroidery on the bed skirt, the room strove for elegance, and succeeded admirably. Elizabeth wondered if all of the private chambers were thus appointed, and why such good taste didn't prevail throughout the dwelling.

After a thorough inspection, she put away her few possessions and then seated herself at the writing desk. Both desk and chair were a bit tall for her, but she knew she was slightly lacking in stature. She was accustomed to encountering the occasional pieces of furniture that emphasized her lack of height.

The desk was well stocked. Elizabeth wrote to her parents, telling them of her change in circumstance and asking their permission to stay at Rosings "while Miss de Bourgh needs me or until you need me at home." She made no reference to Anne's offer to pay her, but did bring up the pocket money, suggesting her father no longer needed to send hers. She made no mention of Mr. Darcy at all.

Her letter to Jane, who was staying with their aunt and uncle in London, was more detailed but still didn't reveal everything. She wasn't quite certain if it was shame, anger or discretion that kept her silent on her exchange with Mr. Darcy and his letter, but she couldn't bear the idea of putting it to page. That meant she also couldn't disclose what she'd learned of Mr. Wickham. She wasn't even tempted to mention Bingley's reason for leaving Netherfield, for she had to agree that, had his love been firm, he wouldn't have been so easily swayed. In the end, she wrote Jane quite a bit about quite little, the letter leaving her rather dissatisfied.

Once she was done, she dressed for dinner. She was about to leave her room in search of a footman to post her letters for her when a knock sounded at the door. She opened it to find Mrs. Jenkinson without.

"Mrs. Jenkinson," Elizabeth greeted, surprised. As she said the woman's name, she realized there was potentially great awkwardness between them. Elizabeth was all but usurping the other woman's place in the household.

"May I come in, Miss Bennet?" Mrs. Jenkinson said.

"Of course." Elizabeth backed into the room.

Mrs. Jenkinson entered and closed the door behind her. She looked around the room before turning to Elizabeth. "Lady Catherine never would give me this room. I always said I wanted it to be closer to Miss de Bourgh, because of her health, but in truth, it's the nicest room. Everything isn't gilded and dripping with gold lame like the rest of the furnishings."

"It's not my intention to displace you," Elizabeth said, feeling no need to mince words.

"I know that," Mrs. Jenkinson said. She smiled, easing Elizabeth's discomfort. "I always knew I would leave as soon as Lady Catherine died. Miss de Bourgh is being very generous and she has set it up so my pension will continue for my lifetime, regardless of what she does or what happens with this estate. I should also be in Lady Catherine's will, being her servant. It's good of Miss de Bourgh to see I'm well provided for even without knowing what's in her mother's will."

"I didn't know you were in Lady Catherine's employ," Elizabeth said. Anne's comments from earlier came back to her and she realized she should have guessed. Why else would Mrs. Jenkinson spy for Lady Catherine, and why else would Anne have kept her on for so long, knowing what she was doing? She wouldn't have, was the obvious answer.

"I was very aware of it, as was Miss de Bourgh. I'm not certain Lady Catherine really understood how difficult that made it for both of us. Be good to her. I did what my employer wanted me to do, but I did my best for Miss de Bourgh as well. I even looked the other way about a few things."

"Midnight reading?" Elizabeth guessed, smiling.

Mrs. Jenkinson chuckled. "I think Miss de Bourgh and Lady Catherine were the only two people at Rosings who weren't aware it was public knowledge."

"Mr. Darcy and Colonel Fitzwilliam knew?" Elizabeth was a bit surprised by that. Mr. Darcy seemed stern enough to try to curtail the activity, for the sake of Anne's health.

"I should rephrase what I just said. All of the servants knew. They kept quiet because Miss de Bourgh was generous." She eyed Elizabeth in a speculative way. "They also felt sorry for Miss de Bourgh," she added. Her smile turned sad. "I'll miss it here. Being a servant at Rosings wasn't bad."

"You weren't--"

"I was a servant," Mrs. Jenkinson said, interrupting Elizabeth's protest. "I have few illusions. I was a servant, even though as a governess and companion I was considered almost part of the family. Almost. Miss de Bourgh means to treat you differently. I hope, for both of your sakes, you will stand up for her and if necessary, to her. Without her mother, I don't think anyone knows how she will behave, least of all her. She can't stay as she was unless she quickly marries a husband who will make all of her decisions for her, and I don't think any good would really come of that."

"Thank you for your understanding, and your advice," Elizabeth said, meaning it. "When did you plan to leave? Before you go, I would like to learn something from you about the workings of Rosings."

"I haven't made arrangements yet, but there's no time like the present," Mrs. Jenkinson said. She smiled wryly and nodded toward the writing desk. "Why don't you sit at the desk? I suggest you take notes."

Chapter Three

Colonel Richard Fitzwilliam climbed into Darcy's carriage, settling into the seat across from him. He was dressed in black, though nothing else about him was notably somber. He nodded to Darcy. "Good of you to give me a ride."

"We're going to the same place," Darcy said. He knocked on the roof and Alderson, his driver, started the carriage moving.

"Who would have thought we'd be returning so soon?" Richard said. "Aunt Catherine was tough as nails. She seemed in fine fettle, too."

"They think it was her heart," Darcy said, although he was sure Richard had received the same information he had.

"I was surprised to learn she had one," Richard muttered.

Darcy didn't smile. He wouldn't pretend deep mourning, as he wasn't much saddened by his aunt's death, but he did think some decorum was in order. Besides, the joke hadn't been amusing and likely wouldn't ever be, no matter how many Fitzwilliams uttered it.

That they would, Darcy was sure. The Fitzwilliams would have all been summoned. They would descend on Rosings and fill Anne's home with a level of boisterousness bordering on crass. Darcy was sorry he would be forced to endure it. He didn't think Anne would fare well.

Darcy turned to watch the passing scenery, not in the mood to converse. Normally, Richard was the most tolerable of Darcy's cousins, aside from Anne. Anne was easy to be around, though not because of any great affection between them. They, neither of them, preferred to speak, and so could keep each other quiet company.

At least, Darcy hoped their ease didn't stem from any affection on Anne's part, because he bore her no more than cousinly regard. One of the reasons he didn't mourn his aunt's passing was the cessation of her ongoing, embarrassingly blatant attempts to force him to propose to Anne. He hoped Anne realized he didn't hold her in that light and hadn't simply been waiting for her mother to die. He wanted to help her keep Rosings in order and deal with their uncle, but he'd have to take care to assess her feelings toward him before he was too adamant on her behalf.

"Did they say who was with her?" Richard asked.

"I beg your pardon?" Darcy asked, turning to his cousin.

"Aunt Catherine," Richard said. "Did they say who was with her when she fell ill?"

"I don't believe it was mentioned, no."

"I wager it was that Miss Bennet. Beguiling girl, but she has a sharp wit. She probably said something that put Aunt Catherine over the edge."

"Don't be ridiculous," Darcy snapped. He turned back to the window, aware he was showing too much temper. It was in poor taste to suggest that Elizabeth had caused Lady Catherine's death, even in jest. Yes, Elizabeth had a quick wit, but she used it to be amusing and to avoid lying, not to torment elderly women, even ones as exasperating as Lady Catherine had been. Darcy had witnessed Elizabeth's expert handling of his aunt and been impressed.

Elizabeth, he thought, letting out a silent sigh. Would she still be in Kent? Even if she was, he wouldn't see her. She wasn't the sort of person his family would invite to dine with them in their time of mourning. She was no one, really. The daughter of a man who hardly maintained the title of gentleman and of a woman whose family was in trade. Elizabeth Bennet was barely even a member of the gentry.

Added to her low status was that, for all of her wit, she wasn't intelligent enough to recognize the greatest opportunity of her life; his proposal. He would have elevated her. She would have wanted for nothing. He would even have taken care of her mother and sisters, so long as he never had to see them.

Darcy frowned out the window. It was all so beneath him. He

34

should never have proposed to her. She was a country miss without fashion or accomplishments. That she hadn't appreciated what he had to offer only showed her lack of taste.

Hopefully she had, at least, been intelligent enough to believe his letter. He couldn't abide the idea that she'd been taken in by Wickham and might still be under his spell. Was he the only person who could see through George Wickham's lies? In Elizabeth's defense, Darcy's own father and sister had both succumbed to Wickham's charms. How could Elizabeth, who knew Wickham much less well than Georgiana and their father, be expected to see through him?

He wished she had, though. He wished she'd seen Wickham as false, and been astute enough to see . . . see what? See the goodness in Darcy's soul? See the truth of his love for her? If she'd seen into his heart well enough to see those things, she'd also have seen his disdain for her family, his embarrassment for her status and, worse, his certainty she would say yes to his proposal simply to elevate herself. He shook his head slightly, aware of how undignified his thoughts were. Elizabeth was right. He seemed to think so little of her, of where she came from, and of women in general, that there was no reason she, or any woman, should fall in love with him.

If only he could as easily remove Elizabeth Bennet from his thoughts as he'd removed himself from her presence. Yet, headed back to Kent as they were, he was aware of a deep longing to see her again. An almost painful hope that she would still be there and her opinion of him would be changed.

He wanted to fence with her again. He wanted to hear one of her clever remarks. He wanted to see her eyes light with humor and warmth. He knew he'd misinterpreted that warmth. It wasn't warmth for him. It may have been warmth against him or for the argument. Whatever it was, it drew him to her.

How could he have misunderstood her so completely? The clues had been there. They weren't even clues, but statements. She was always polite, but she criticized him. Yet she did so enchantingly, and justly. That was what stung the most. Her reproofs had merit.

The carriage pulled up, coming to an abrupt stop and mercifully pulling Darcy from a too familiar spiral of inner turmoil. He threw the door open and jumped out, not caring at first why they'd stopped. He was happy to be jolted from the disorder in his mind, and heart.

"Darcy, what's the trouble?" Richard called, leaning out the door.

Darcy shook his head, not answering, and looked to his aged driver, who was climbing down from the seat. "Alderson?"

"I think one of the horses threw a shoe, sir," Alderson said. He walked up to the horse in question, leaning against it and running a hand down its foreleg so it would lift its hoof. "Yup, thrown a shoe, sir. We'll have to walk 'um till we can come to a town with a smith."

"Fine," Darcy said, ignoring the mild curse Richard muttered. The next town wasn't near, nor was the previous. Darcy climbed back into the carriage, resigning himself to hours of listening to his own unproductive thoughts.

"If you were traveling with your usual entourage, we could switch carriages," Richard said, referring to Darcy's typical cases, valet and other servants, usually allotted their own carriage for longer trips.

"Stevens won't be along for several days," Darcy said, referring to his valet. He saw no reason to expound on that, ignoring Richard's raised brow. The truth was, his valet's wife had recently granted the man a son and Darcy had given him several days leave. Darcy was only to wear black, after all, and perfectly capable of dressing himself. The staff at Rosings could attend to his needs. Most gentlemen didn't encourage their hired men to have families, often sacking them for doing so, but Darcy had always found that a man with a family was a more stable sort of person. For stability and loyalty, he was more than willing to put up with the occasional inconvenience to his person.

By the time they found a blacksmith, he'd already let his coals cool for the day. Darcy had to pay extra to get him to rekindle the fire. He would have rented a team instead, but there weren't any to be had.

"At least we've plenty of time for dinner," Richard said as they seated themselves in a private room at the only inn the town had to offer, to wait on the smith.

His tone was light. Darcy suspected his cousin was perfectly aware of his dark mood. He sighed, deliberately forcing his mind away from Kent and the possibility of seeing Elizabeth. Richard was making every effort to be a pleasant travel companion, and it behooved Darcy to act in kind.

It turned out they had excessive time for a leisurely dinner, which, Darcy had to admit, wasn't bad. Hearty would be the most appropriate word for the fare, and it was better than was typical of the sort of establishment. Once the forge was fired up, Alderson checked all fifteen other shoes on the team, deeming that two more needed replacing. Darcy rather thought that was something his driver should have done before embarking on the trip, but he knew he'd been in a hurry to leave and hadn't given the man time.

Even with the long hours of May daylight, it was after dark when they arrived as Rosings. Darcy had rarely been so pleased to see the place and he knew it wasn't only because the journey had been long. Rosings seemed somehow less grim than usual. He wasn't sure if he should account the feeling to knowing his aunt wasn't waiting to torment him, or to his memories of spending time there with Elizabeth.

He and Richard both disembarked as soon as the carriage came near to a halt. Darcy suspected his cousin was as eager to leave the cramped interior as he. They jogged up the steps side by side, to be greeted by a footman.

"Miss de Bourgh has already retired, sirs," the man said.

Darcy nodded and headed for the staircase.

"Thank you," he heard Richard say behind him. "I was wondering if you could have a nightcap sent up for me?"

"Yes, Colonel," the footman said. "I'll see to it in a moment. If you'll excuse me, I must . . ."

Darcy lost whatever else the footman had to say. He was eager to gain the sanctuary of his room. It was a weakness, he knew, but hours spent in company wore on him like a slow torture. Even if the company was one of his closest companions, as Richard was. A flaw in his character, to be sure, but one he didn't feel the need to rectify at that moment.

Of course, there was one person whose company never seemed to tire him. Rather the opposite. Her, he could spend days with . . . and nights. A smile slipped across his face as he reached the refuge of his usual room and opened the door, his mind flirting with the idea of nights with—

"Elizabeth?" Darcy said, stunned into immobility where he stood on the threshold of his room, the door half open.

"Mr. Darcy," she gasped, snatching up a quilt to clutch before her nightgown-clad form.

Darcy immediately swung the door closed. He stood there, shocked. Elizabeth Bennet. In his room. In a state of undress.

"Sir," a voice called from the end of the hall.

Darcy turned his head to see the footman who'd greeted them, looking frazzled.

"Sir, don't open the door," the man gasped, hurrying down the hall. "That room has been given to Miss Bennet, at Miss de Bourgh's request."

Darcy looked down at his hand, finding it still on the latch. He pulled it back, realizing the footman had no idea he was already too late. If the man had come a few seconds earlier . . . Darcy turned from the door, schooling his features into a frown. "Miss Bennet is staying here?"

"Yes, sir, at Miss de Bourgh's invitation," the footman said. "A room was prepared for you this way, sir."

He gestured, turning down the hall. Darcy followed automatically, the image of Elizabeth in her nightgown, her hair in a single braid down her back, etched into his vision. Did she leave it braided while she slept, or did she free it to spread out about her head, draping her pillow in luxurious dark strands?

38

"This room, sir," the footman said, jolting Darcy back to reality in time to keep from walking into him.

"Thank you," Darcy said. "That will be all."

The footman bowed and turned away. Darcy let himself into the room, finding it smaller than the one he was accustomed to and too ornate. It had taken him years to maneuver furnishings he cared for into his usual room. What was Elizabeth doing in it? What was she doing in Rosings at all?

He stuck his head back out into the hallway, but the footman was long gone. Likely, the man wouldn't know the answers to Darcy's question anyhow and it wouldn't really be appropriate to ask. He closed the door again and began to undress. He would have to wait until morning to learn what was transpiring. One thing was certain, though: With the image of Elizabeth standing beside his bed in her nightgown seared into his mind, it was going to be a long night.

Chapter Four

The following morning Darcy sat in his room waiting for the hour he knew Richard preferred to dine. Darcy suspected Elizabeth was the type to breakfast early and he didn't want to add to the awkwardness of the incident the night before by forcing her to be alone with him. Not that any encounter with her wouldn't be awkward, the night before having only added to the list of shared secrets between them.

He felt the decided need to apologize for walking in on her and to explain that the room was normally reserved for him. He didn't know if she would welcome him referencing the incident, however, even to apologize. He also didn't know if she would be comfortable being alone with a man who'd both proposed to her and opened her bedroom door unannounced, but it wasn't an apology that could be made in public. Not unless he wanted to force her to marry him.

He amused himself by toying with that idea until he heard the tread of Richard's boot-shod feet in the hall. Crossing to the door of his room, Darcy placed the idea of manipulating Elizabeth into marrying him firmly out of his mind, where it belonged. He opened the door to a moderately surprised looking Richard and stepped out into the hall.

"A bit late for you, isn't it?" Richard asked as Darcy fell in step with him.

"Yesterday was a long day," Darcy said.

"I know. I was there, you'll recall."

Darcy nodded, not feeling that was meant to be replied to.

"That wasn't your usual room," Richard said. "Anne set you in your place, has she?"

Darcy shrugged, definitely not wanting to go into any details about rooms.

41

"Good thing is, it shows she was never serious about that idea of you proposing. Wouldn't have moved you down so many doors if she was."

Darcy frowned. They were nearing the breakfast parlor. Richard's choice of topics was questionable under any circumstances, but doubly unacceptable when someone might overhear them. He turned a repressive glare on the colonel, only to find Richard wasn't looking his way.

"Miss Bennet, what a pleasant surprise," Richard said as they entered the breakfast parlor.

Darcy forced his eyes to go to Anne, who was looking weary and drawn. "Anne, Mrs. Jenkinson, Miss Bennet," he said. He turned immediately to the sideboard, finding himself unable to look at Elizabeth without picturing her as he'd seen her the night before.

"Richard, Darcy," he hear Anne say behind him. Neither Elizabeth nor Anne's companion spoke.

"Anne, dearest cousin," Richard said. "My heartfelt condolences on your loss."

"Thank you, Richard," Anne said.

Darcy winced, realizing he should have delivered a similar condolence. He'd already begun to assemble food on a plate, though. It would have to wait until he sat.

"It surprises me to find you here, Miss Bennet, and in black as well," Richard continued. "You couldn't have had such a gown with you for the occasion."

"It's one of Lady Catherine's gowns," Elizabeth said. "Miss de Bourgh insisted I wear it. It took quite the combined effort to make the conversion."

"Elizabeth was very clever about it," Anne said. "She managed to save several seams so we didn't have to redo them all."

Darcy closed his eyes for a moment, breathing in slowly, before willing all expression from his face and turning around.

"It's Anne who we should have fitted it for," Elizabeth said. "She'll need to wear black for quite some time."

She was every bit as enchanting as he recalled, even in unrelenting black. Darcy walked toward the table, realizing Richard had taken the seat across from Elizabeth, leaving him only one choice, to sit beside her or take a seat farther down the table and appear deliberately rude. He deposited his plate at the setting next to Elizabeth and spoke to Anne. "I'm very sorry for the loss of your mother."

She looked up at him through tired eyes. "Thank you, Darcy." Anne gave him a sad smile and turned back to the others, freeing him to take his seat. "I need an entirely new wardrobe of black. There was nothing to be gained by modifying one dress for my sake. Besides, it was a chance to do something for you, Elizabeth."

"I don't mean to pry, cousin, or come across as displeased to see the lovely Miss Bennet in any way, but why is she here?" Richard asked. He turned to look at Elizabeth. "I can't believe you've grown so found of my aunt that you're here solely to mourn her."

"Indeed, while I sincerely mourn for Anne's loss, I can claim no greater affection sprang up between Lady Catherine and me after you departed than existed before," Elizabeth said.

Darcy sipped his coffee to hide his smile. He'd missed her evasive answers, sweet sounding but with a core of hard truth. Elizabeth turned away from Richard, looking to Anne, and Darcy realized she was wondering if his cousin would provide an answer to Richard's real question.

"I asked Elizabeth to stay for a time," Anne said. "I feel the need of her opinion on several matters."

Interesting, Darcy thought. What of his opinion, or Richard's? Apparently, Elizabeth's thoughts were more valuable, or at least equally so. Darcy could concur with that, but he was surprised Anne had come to the idea.

"And what of you, Richard?" Anne said. "I hope this summons was not too inconvenient, with you only just having been away."

Richard started into a familiar diatribe about the life of an officer,

Anne's questions encouraging him. In spite of her haggard appearance, Darcy hadn't seen his cousin so animated since she was a child. He didn't know how much of Anne's loquaciousness was due to Elizabeth's influence and how much came from the absence of her domineering mother, but he was pleased to see it. Anne would have the running of Rosings, after all, and would need to assert herself.

As they lingered over what was already a late breakfast, a footman entered the room, bowing. "I beg your pardons, sirs, misses, but a Mr. Hayes is here, Lady Catherine's attorney. He said he wouldn't have come yet if he'd known you weren't through dining and that he can return later."

"Tell him to stay," Darcy said, standing. As much as he was enjoying sitting beside Elizabeth, taking in her occasional remark, he was tired of inactivity. "Richard, with me, if you will."

"Right," Richard said, rising from the table with a lingering look at the remains of his meal. "Ladies," he added with a bow.

Darcy strode from the room, Richard's footsteps following him. Behind them, Darcy could hear the rustle of skirts and murmuring voices. He frowned, sensing displeasure in the tones, though he couldn't make out the words. Shrugging, he realized it likely had little to do with him and lengthened his stride.

He and Richard met with the attorney in Lady Catherine's study. Mr. Hayes was a small and exceedingly elderly gentleman who looked as if he should have passed from life long before their Aunt Catherine. They discussed some of the details of the estate, focusing on the few more pressing issues. Richard remained mostly silent, seeming content to allow Darcy to make any decisions that needed to be made, and Mr. Hayes agreed with everything excessively. It was wearing, but Darcy could only assume it was what his aunt had liked about the man.

After nearly an hour, Hayes seemed satisfied, standing to depart. "One last thing," he said as he gathered up his papers. "When do you wish me to read the will?"

Darcy looked to his cousin, who shrugged. "I believe we should wait for Lady Catherine's brother, Earl of Matlock, to arrive," he said, turning back to Mr. Hayes.

"Most appropriate. Assuredly so," Hayes said, nodding.

Darcy and Richard both stood, shaking the man's hand. As he tottered from the room, Richard shot Darcy an amused look before retaking his seat. The colonel reached for the newspaper on Lady Catherine's desk, likely placed there out of habit. With his cousin occupied, Darcy quit the room, feeling he should provide Anne with a summary of what they'd decided.

A footman directed him to the appropriate parlor where he found Anne, Elizabeth and Mrs. Jenkinson all busily sewing black garments. He was pleased to see them so well employed, but his cousin and Elizabeth both stopped working immediately when he entered. Anne fixed him with a surprisingly stern look.

"Darcy," she said, nodding to him but not standing. "In the future, I would appreciate it if I be included in any meetings with my mother's attorney concerning my estate."

Darcy blinked, caught off guard on the verge of bowing in greeting. "Of course," he said. He cast a glance at Elizabeth, wondering if this was her doing. "I came immediately to tell you what transpired."

"And what did transpire while you, Richard and that little man were deciding what to do with my holdings?"

Darcy tried to rearrange his thoughts. If he didn't know any better, he would say Anne was angry. "We decided not to hold the reading of the will until the Earl of Matlock arrives," he said, grasping at the first detail that came to mind.

"Is the Earl of Matlock in the will?" Elizabeth asked, exchanging a look with Anne.

Darcy frowned. He was right, this was Elizabeth's doing and he was uncertain if he approved. "I don't know."

Elizabeth set aside her sewing and stood up. Darcy stayed where he was, a few feet into the parlor, watching in bewilderment as she crossed the room to ring for a servant. Elizabeth returned to her chair, she and

Anne sitting straight backed and intent looking. Mrs. Jenkinson kept sewing, her face downturned toward her work. In moments, a maid hurried into the room.

"See if you can catch the attorney before he leaves the property," Elizabeth said. "If you can't, send a groom after him."

For a few seconds everything seemed frozen. The maid looked to Darcy, obviously unsure if she should carry out Elizabeth's order. Darcy didn't move, aware he'd somehow placed himself on precarious ground.

"Do it," Anne said, tilting her chin up in an effort to look commanding.

The maid glanced at Anne before turning beseeching eyes back to Darcy. He didn't know what she wanted him to say, but he wasn't foolish enough to embroil himself any further in the issue. True, he and Richard were done speaking with the attorney, but this wasn't Pemberley. Rosings was almost certainly Anne's now, and the maid answered to her.

"I doubt Miss de Bourgh has much of a place in her household for servants who don't obey her orders," Elizabeth said quietly.

The maid was still looking at him. Darcy realized he would have to speak. "Quickly. He can't have gone far," he said. Wide-eyed, the maid scurried from the room. Darcy turned to Elizabeth, choosing his words carefully. "Why would Miss de Bourgh need to see the attorney?"

Elizabeth turned to Anne, but she shook her head, looking suddenly exhausted. "She should know her status as soon as possible," Elizabeth replied.

"She is to inherit Rosings," Darcy said. "It was in her father's will."

"Are there any other bequests?" Elizabeth asked.

Darcy looked between his cousin and Elizabeth. Anne nodded, signaling that he should answer the question. Was this why Anne had asked Elizabeth to stay, to teach her to be more willful? She likely couldn't have found a better role model. "I'm not entirely certain," he admitted.

"I would like to be certain," Anne said in a quiet voice.

"We will be, once the will is read," Darcy said, starting to feel as if he had indeed misstepped. If he were in Anne's place, wouldn't he want to know the parameters of his future? Did he think that Anne being a woman meant she held no concerns over such matters? Lady Catherine, a woman, had run the estate for years.

"Does anyone have any control over Miss de Bourgh's money or her decisions concerning Rosings?" Elizabeth asked, sounding a bit exasperated with his silence.

"No," Mr. Hayes said as he entered the room, saving Darcy from a second embarrassing admission of a lack of full knowledge. "The only thing that constrains her is that she cannot sell Rosings." He looked around the room, his face pinched.

Anne nodded, obviously having expected that constraint. "Nor would I wish to sell Rosings."

"Perhaps it would be a good idea to read the will now," Darcy said, meeting Elizabeth's gaze.

"Without the Earl of Matlock?" Hayes asked.

"Is he mentioned in the will?" Elizabeth asked.

"No," Mr. Hayes said, wringing his hands. "You aren't either, young lady." He straightened his shoulders, glaring at her. "I'm not entirely sure who you are, but there's no reason for you to be there for the reading." Hayes turned to Darcy, his expression that of a hound expecting a reward.

"Miss Bennet is my friend and she will be there," Anne said. Her tone was once again firm, but she looked even paler than before.

"Certainly, Miss de Bourgh," Mr. Hayes said, shrinking in on himself as if Anne had threatened bodily or fiscal harm. "Yes, a splendid idea."

"In Lady Catherine's study, then?" Darcy suggested. He made sure to keep his tone light. He in no way wished his words to sound like an order.

"It's my study now," Anne said, standing.

She swayed slightly. Darcy took a step forward, but Elizabeth was already there, placing an arm about Anne's shoulders. She murmured something too low for him to hear, but Anne shook her head.

"We're hearing the will read now," Anne said, her lips pressed into a firm line. "Darcy, please assist Mr. Hayes in assembling the relevant individuals. Miss Bennet and I will join you soon."

Darcy nodded, not needing the firm look Elizabeth sent his way to persuade him to obey Anne. He understood what Miss Bennet was attempting to accomplish. His cousin was seen as someone with no thoughts of her own, no opinions and certainly no strength. Now, she would have to manage Rosings and likely deal with suitors of the most tenacious type. Elizabeth was trying to help Anne establish that she did indeed have purpose of character and Darcy had no wish to undermine that.

In the end, the reading was moved to a larger room, more of the beneficiaries of the will being readily available than Darcy would have suspected. There were no outlandish surprises. Nearly everything went to Anne, though Colonel Fitzwilliam received two thousand pounds. All of the servants housed at Rosings were awarded sums equal to their entire wages since they'd begun working there. The tenant farmers and workers who lived outside of Rosings were bequeathed amounts equivalent to ten percent of their total earnings. Many of the maids were only paid about five pounds a year and most were young enough that they hadn't worked for very long, so their sums were relatively small, but the most experienced servants were to receive rather large sums.

If anything could be said to have been unexpected, it was that Lady Catherine had turned out to be more generous than Darcy anticipated. When he heard murmurs of how great and kind a lady his aunt had been, Darcy didn't know if he should be amused or disgusted. He was sure such a change in opinion had been paramount in his aunt's decisions.

The reading concluded, Mr. Hayes began to bundle his belongings once more. "Will that be all, then, sir?" he asked, turning to Darcy.

Having learned his lesson, Darcy turned to Anne.

"Will that be all, Miss de Bourgh?" Hayes added hurriedly, becoming nervous once more.

"I would like to put this behind us as quickly as possible," Anne said. "How soon can my mother's commitments be met?"

"There is no one to contest Lady Catherine's wishes. You have full access to her . . . that is *your* funds, Miss de Bourgh," Hayes said. "I can arrange for the money to be made available to you almost immediately."

"See it done," Miss de Bourgh said. "I would like it brought here so that I may disperse it."

"Yes, Miss de Bourgh. An excellent idea," Mr. Hayes said.

Darcy wasn't sure it was an excellent idea. He looked for Elizabeth, who'd been off to the side for the reading, hoping she would recommend against having so much money brought to Rosings so quickly. She was nowhere to be seen, however.

Chapter Five

Elizabeth stood to one side of the room, feeling out of place. She really didn't have any reason to be there for the reading of the will, as the attorney had pointed out. She also felt awkward being anywhere within sight of Mr. Darcy. It was exceedingly difficult to keep her jumble of emotions concerning him at bay when he was right there looking so very domineering and undeniably handsome. It had been bad enough thinking of him far away and in want of an apology from her, yet still the object of her anger. Adding him near and seeing her in nothing but a nightgown the evening before was simply too much. She couldn't undermine Anne by declining to attend, though, and so kept her eyes downcast and away from Mr. Darcy's face.

As soon as the official reading was over, a servant approached her with letters from her Aunt Gardiner and Jane. A glance showed her that Mr. Darcy was with Anne, speaking with the attorney. Feeling he could be relied on to curtail any foolish decisions, Elizabeth slipped away. She smiled in anticipation of hearing from two of her favorite people.

She wandered back to the parlor they'd been sewing in, opening Jane's letter as soon as she sat down.

My dearest Lizzy,

I'm afraid you were correct. I never did see Miss Bingley again. Nor did I see Mr. Bingley, even once. I don't mind, though, for I am quite over him. I'm sure I never held him in so much esteem as I first thought. It was merely the dancing, and the laughing, that convinced me I held such high affection. Now that we have neither danced nor laughed together for so long, I can set any lingering sentiment aside. I will remember him as the most pleasing

man I've ever known, and I am certain he never intended
anything serious. He can't be blamed for attracting me
because he is so attractive.

Oh Jane, Elizabeth thought, sighing. She cast a glare over her shoulder in the general direction of Mr. Darcy, even though it was through a wall. She could sense the sorrow hidden in Jane's calm words. If she was sure in which direction the duplicitous Miss Bingley lay, she would cast a glare toward her as well. Instead, she returned her eyes to the page.

I am ever so happy to be home, as London was quite
busy. Much as I enjoyed being with my aunt and uncle in
London, I missed Hertfordshire. Now that I've been away
from Mr. Bingley for so long, I am sure that I will be able to
look at the places where I spent time with him without there
being a constant reminder of him.

Elizabeth smiled sadly. Every line Jane wrote to convince Elizabeth that she was no longer sad about Mr. Bingley's desertion instead convinced her that Jane was still deeply in love with him. She continued reading, scanning predictable lines about her mother, the neighbors, and Kitty, her smile still in place until she reached a section about Lydia.

I'm sure Father will permit you to stay in Kent. He has
permitted Lydia to journey to Brighton as a friend to Colonel
Forster's wife and so can hardly have grounds to deny you. I
harbor some concern about Lydia being away from family
while she is still so young, but if Colonel Forster can
command the militia in Meryton without any problems with
the local population, he surely can take care of a girl who is
not quite sixteen.

Kitty is devastated not to be allowed to go. She's
pointed out that she's the older of the two so many times,
it's starting to grow tiresome. I do feel for her, though. It's
an unhappy thing to be left behind.

The unhappy thing was their father permitting Lydia to go at all,

Elizabeth thought. How could he consent to it? Nothing good could come from Lydia being in Brighton with a whole campful of soldiers and no one likely to restrain her.

Elizabeth was filled with such a dire feeling by the news, she could hardly attend to the rest of Jane's letter. She refolded it, setting aside the normally welcome details of home to read later, once her nerves were settled. She tried to assure herself that the wife of a colonel must be a responsible person, though Mrs. Forster's preference for Lydia's company gainsaid that notion.

She opened her aunt's letter, hoping for something to distract her from her concern over Lydia.

Dear Elizabeth,

I hope this letter finds you well. It's my understanding you're still in Kent. As I have every reason to assume Mr. Bennet will permit you to remain there for the foreseeable future, that is where I've written you. If I was mistaken and you don't receive this letter for some time, I can only hope it has caught up to your travels.

Your uncle and I are soon to embark on a pleasure tour of the Lakes. It was our intension that you should accompany us. As you're otherwise engaged, we shall invite your sister Mary. I would have enjoyed your company, but I think the trip will benefit Mary. It may be that taking in more of the world will alter her in some small, becoming way.

Elizabeth frowned, then quickly looked about the room to ensure no one was there to witness it. It wasn't that she was ungrateful for Miss de Bourgh's friendship, but she would very much have liked to tour the Lakes with her favorite aunt and uncle. Her aunt was likely correct, though, that it would benefit Mary. Being the middle sister, Mary was often left out. Not only the culture of the trip, but being allowed something special and the undivided attention of their aunt and uncle may well do Mary some much needed good.

Having made up her mind that it was indeed for the best that Mary be awarded the indulgence, Elizabeth returned to reading. She was in the middle of a long paragraph concerning her young cousins when footfalls sounded in the hall. She looked up as Anne, Mrs. Jenkinson, Colonel Fitzwilliam and Mr. Darcy entered the room.

". . .unsurprised," Anne was saying. "It was all as I expected. I inherit everything except for minor bequests."

Colonel Fitzwilliam turned a wry smile on her. "It shows your wealth that you consider two thousand pounds to be minor."

"My mother was grateful to you and Darcy for helping her with the estate," Anne said, retaking her customary seat on the settee across from the door.

Colonel Fitzwilliam bowed to her. "One helps family, of course. Although it wasn't difficult. Your mother's steward does a good job of managing Rosings."

He seated himself opposite Elizabeth, unfurling the newspaper he held. Mrs. Jenkinson returned to her customary place, taking up her sewing. Mr. Darcy bowed to Elizabeth and took the chair beside hers, sending a thrill of nerves through her with his nearness. Telling herself that Mr. Darcy was too much of a gentleman to hold the image of her in a state of undress in his mind, Elizabeth tamped down her disquiet. She carefully folded her aunt's letter to finish reading later at her leisure.

Before anyone could initiate conversation, a maid appeared in the doorway to announce Mr. Collins. Elizabeth looked around the room and saw that no one was happy to see him, including Anne.

"Miss de Bourgh, I cannot express how concerned I am about your terrible loss. I—"

"Mr. Collins," Anne said.

"—was stunned, to be sure. Of course, you will wish my advice in this time of need. I make myself and my wife wholly available to you. I cannot tell you how devastated we both are. I offer you every condolence and—"

"Mr. Collins!" Anne reiterated, louder than before.

Mr. Collins stopped speaking, his mouth hanging open for a moment before he snapped it closed, a look of confusion slackening his features.

"You have expressed your concern to me every time you've seen me," Anne said. "I don't want to hear it again."

"But I am your spiritual advisor. You need my help and suppo—"

"Mr. Collins!" Anne exclaimed.

He stopped speaking, his eyes going wide.

"I will listen to your sermons every Sunday, but I am tired of having you here," Anne said. "You can please me best by not coming unless you are invited. Mrs. Collins is always welcome, so long as you don't send her here. Nor should you ever impede her from coming. I suggest that you learn to listen to your wife. She knows best in this case. Be content with the support you gave to my mother."

He stood there with an expression of astonishment on his face.

"Go!" Anne said.

Mr. Collins looked first at Mr. Darcy who gave him a nod. He looked at Colonel Fitzwilliam who said, "I'm not going to argue. A soldier knows who is in command."

Elizabeth took pity on him, partly because she thought Anne was being too harsh after the attention Lady Catherine had given him. "Miss de Bourgh wants only her relatives and women with her now," she told him.

"I am grateful that your cousin Elizabeth is here," Anne said. "You have given me someone to lean on. Let that be enough."

Mr. Collins stood for a moment longer, looking bereft. Finally, he bowed and backed from the room, casting them beseeching glances until his feet carried him from view.

"That was tactful," Elizabeth said, though she meant only the last of Anne's words to her cousin.

Anne sighed. "Your words made me realize I shouldn't be too harsh with him. He behaves how my mother wanted him to behave. I shouldn't be mad at him for that, but I can't stand the man."

55

"Are you ever going to invite him here again?" Darcy asked.

"For his wife's sake, every couple of months. If I can train him to be quiet, maybe more often," Anne replied. She turned to Elizabeth. "Did I do the right thing?"

"Yes," she said. "Both in telling him to go if you don't want him here and in trying to do it in a kind way."

"Well then," Anne said. "I'm going to tell my butler I will not be receiving anyone, even for condolence calls. I do not want to sit through my neighbors telling me how sorry they are for my mother's death when they didn't like her." She looked at Elizabeth. "I'll have him tell people I am not up to seeing visitors."

"That would be a better way of saying it," Elizabeth said with a smile, though still probably not good. If Anne wanted to function as mistress of Rosings, she would have to learn to mix with her neighbors. Elizabeth knew that in a farming community, farmers frequently exchanged valuable information. On the other hand, perhaps Anne's steward would make all of the decisions relating to the farm. She opened her mouth to comment.

"I see you have letters," Anne said, a slightly beseeching look on her face. "Have you heard anything from your father yet?"

Elizabeth realized Anne didn't wish to discuss the topic of visiting neighbors any further and decided it would wait for another time. "No, but I did receive opinions that he is likely to assent."

"Was there anything else of interest in the letters?" Anne asked, picking up her sewing.

"My sister Mary is to go on a tour of the Lakes with my aunt and uncle, the Gardiners," she said. She cast a glance at Mr. Darcy and resolved not to mention Jane. "My youngest sister, Lydia, will be traveling as well. She's to go to Brighton with a Colonel and Mrs. Forster."

As soon as she said it, Elizabeth wished she hadn't. It was hardly private news, but the mere mention of it set her nerves knotting. What was her father thinking? At least her tone hadn't given away her worry

56

over Lydia, or her envy of Mary. She hoped.

"I remember you told my mother you have four sisters," Anne said as she measured out a length of thread.

"I do," Elizabeth said. She knew she ought to be sewing as well, like Mrs. Jenkinson and Anne, but her nerves would turn what was a moderate skill into an absolute disaster. Besides, Mr. Darcy was doing nothing save attending to the conversation, so she could emulate him without the appearance of idleness.

"Your eldest sister spent the winter in London, I believe," Anne said. "You are here. Your youngest sister is to travel to Brighton. Is Mary the second youngest or the middle child?"

"Mary follows me," Elizabeth said, wondering at Anne's curiosity for a moment before she recalled the promise of letting her sisters visit. She hadn't realized Anne would think of it again so soon. "Then Kitty, then Lydia."

"So only the second youngest, Kitty, will have had no travel?

"Correct," Elizabeth said. "Her name is actually Catherine, of course. We only call her Kitty."

"Can't imagine anyone calling our Aunt Catherine that," Colonel Fitzwilliam mumbled behind his newspaper.

Elizabeth suppressed a smile. Nor could she imagine anyone addressing Lady Catherine as such. Lady Kitty. She covered her mouth and coughed to hide the laugh that tried to escape.

"If your father gives you permission to stay here, would it be acceptable if I invite your sister Kitty to join us?" Anne asked, either not hearing or choosing to ignore the colonel. "It won't be very exciting, but at least it will give her a chance to see another part of the world."

"That's very kind of you," Elizabeth said.

Although it was Jane she'd hoped to invite, Elizabeth didn't see any reason to deny Kitty the opportunity. She wasn't sure she would like having Jane there so long as Mr. Darcy remained, anyhow. He was a constant reminder of Mr. Bingley. It could only sadden Jane and increase Elizabeth's anger to have them near one another. Kitty wouldn't find a visit to Rosings to be much of a treat, but it was something to do while Lydia was in Brighton.

That would leave Jane home alone with their mother and father. Perhaps it would be soothing for the whole household. Hopefully it wouldn't amount to torture for Jane, being the only available focus for their mother. If Elizabeth remained with Anne for a few months, she could always invite Jane next, assuming her hostess proved willing.

The next day's mail brought a letter from Elizabeth's father. She, Anne and Mrs. Jenkinson were again seated in the parlor working on Anne's wardrobe, though Elizabeth wished it otherwise. She was bored with sewing, never an invigorating task, and tired of being quiet and still. She longed for a brisk walk and fresh air, two things Anne never seemed to desire.

There was also a letter for Colonel Fitzwilliam, but he and Mr. Darcy were out riding. Though not much of an equestrian, Elizabeth envied them the ability to go where they pleased and not be confined to be within walking distance. Setting aside her sewing, she opened the letter from her father. She had the fleeting, uncharitable hope that his permission wouldn't be forthcoming.

> Dear Elizabeth,
>
> Though Jane is here, our home wants you to balance out the silliness that still remains. Unfortunately, it seems you are needed where you are. Stay for so long as you are pleased to stay and feel yourself required, but not a moment past.
>
> Your Loving Father

"Is it from your father?" Anne asked as Elizabeth scanned the short message a second time. "What does he say?"

"He says I may remain as long as I wish and am needed," she said, trying to sound pleased. Seeing her father's hand made her miss him and her home in a way that Jane's agitating letter had not.

"That's wonderful news," Anne said. "Mrs. Jenkinson, could you please ring for a servant and request my writing supplies be brought? I wish to write Mr. Bennet immediately to inquire about inviting Miss Kitty."

"Of course," Mrs. Jenkinson said.

Though she gave no indication by tone or manner that she resented the request, it reminded Elizabeth of when Mrs. Jenkinson had insisted she was more of a servant there than a true companion. Once Mrs. Jenkinson left, which she likely would when Mrs. Allen arrived, would Elizabeth be thrust into a servant's role? Elizabeth didn't care for the notion of being treated as a servant by Anne, or anyone.

Anne's letter was written and sent off with a footman by the time Colonel Fitzwilliam and Mr. Darcy returned. The colonel accepted his correspondence and sank into a chair with a sigh, but Mr. Darcy strode across the room as if invigorated by hours in the saddle, rather than taxed. Though she tried not to, Elizabeth couldn't help but notice how well he looked in his riding clothes, his eyes alive and his skin darkened slightly by the sun.

"Blast it all," Colonel Fitzwilliam said.

Elizabeth wrenched her eyes from Mr. Darcy, turning to see Colonel Fitzwilliam surge to his feet. He strode across the room toward her, his expression grim. For an alarmed moment, Elizabeth wondered what she could possibly have done, but realized the colonel's goal was Mr. Darcy, who'd somehow ended up standing before her. He turned now to his cousin.

"Read this, Darcy." Colonel Fitzwilliam thrust the letter at Mr. Darcy and started pacing the room, muttering curses under his breath.

"I'm sorry to hear it," Darcy said, looking up from the letter.

"I shall have to depart at once, of course," Colonel Fitzwilliam said.

"Whatever is the matter?" Anne asked, sounding alarmed.

Mr. Darcy looked to the colonel.

"It's father," Colonel Fitzwilliam said. "He was dashing about the house for some reason and took a tumble. They say his left arm is broken and he knocked his head. So far he's alive, but they can't get the old dog to wake up."

Mr. Darcy held out the letter. Colonel Fitzwilliam waved it off. He wheeled around, bowing in Anne's general direction. "Ladies," he said, hurrying from the room.

Elizabeth could hear him calling for a fresh horse. Mr. Darcy turned back toward her, his expression worried. He sat in the chair beside hers and carefully folded the letter.

"Oh my," Anne said. "I hope Uncle Matlock will recover."

Mr. Darcy nodded, looking grim.

Chapter Six

Darcy woke with a heavy heart and dressed slowly, tired of donning unrelenting black. At his suggestion, they were holding the funeral that morning. None of the Fitzwilliams would be able to attend with the earl so unwell. There was no reason to delay any longer.

As he stood before the mirror carefully tying his cravat, Darcy hoped his uncle would recover and he could soon put off his mourning clothes, as soon as it was decent for him to do so for his aunt. Although if his uncle died, it would not extend the period of mourning by much. Darcy wasn't given to bleak or maudlin thoughts but his mother and father were already gone, and his Aunt Catherine and Uncle Lewis. It was too soon for Matlock to follow.

He let his hands fall and studied his appearance, finding it satisfactory both to himself and propriety. Briefly, he allowed himself to picture Elizabeth at his side and it occurred to him that he was too tall. He'd never thought so before, being secretly pleased with his stature, but perhaps it was something she didn't like about him. She would have to crane her neck to look up at him, after all, when she was standing close. Darcy shook his head, exerting all of his will to drive thoughts of Elizabeth from his mind and properly attend to the obligations of the morning.

The funeral was a dreary affair, as was to be expected. He couldn't help but wish to be riding instead. A man needed freedom and fresh air to clear his head and assuage his grief, though he knew he grieved more for the oftentimes cruelness that was life than for Lady Catherine herself.

Later, his duties finally met, Darcy made his way to Anne's favorite parlor to find her, Elizabeth and Mrs. Jenkinson sewing, as usual. What wasn't usual was that the material they worked on was a stunning blue color, not black. He sank wearily into the chair nearest Elizabeth and asked, "Blue?"

"For Elizabeth," Anne said, looking up. Her eyes were sympathetic and he realized she must be aware he'd had a tiring day thus far. "She needn't always wear black."

"It's another of Lady Catherine's dresses," Elizabeth said. "Miss de Bourgh is very generous, though I worry she's too hasty to give her mother's things away."

"We must put her death behind us," Anne said. "No good will come from enshrining perfectly good material. Speaking of which, there's another task that needs completing today. Mrs. Jenkinson, could you ring for a maid?"

"Yes, of course," Mrs. Jenkinson said, standing.

Darcy frowned. He wouldn't have noticed it if Elizabeth's face hadn't taken on a disapproving look, which she quickly hid, but Anne did seem to order her companion about a great deal. Mrs. Jenkinson wasn't actually a servant, after all. She was a gentlewoman.

He shrugged, leaning back in his chair and watching Elizabeth's hands as she sewed. She had long, delicate, capable fingers and created a very even stitch. Still, skilled as she was at it, she must be growing tired of sewing. In fact, it had been his intention the afternoon before to invite her for a walk, as the day had been very fine. Of course, Richard's news had spoiled that plan. Maybe this afternoon, though, when Anne was through with whatever it was she'd requested a maid for.

"You rang, misses, sir?" a girl said, stepping into the room.

"Yes," Anne said, looking up. "Please tell Mrs. Barclay and Mr. Greyson that I would like to see them."

"Yes, miss," the maid said.

As the girl hurried away, Anne set her sewing aside, sitting up straighter and smoothing her black skirts.

Darcy frowned, wondering why she wished to see her housekeeper and chief steward. "Anne?"

"I'm seeing that my mother's will is carried out, Darcy," she said, not looking at him. Her face had a resolute cast.

Elizabeth's hands stilled. She looked up at Darcy in mild alarm, her face questioning. Mrs. Barclay and Mr. Greyson entered the parlor.

"You sent for us, miss?" Mr. Greyson said, bowing.

Mrs. Barclay curtsied.

Anne nodded. "Please see that all of the household staff and the farm workers are gathered. It is time to give out the bequests from Lady Catherine. Anyone who wants to leave before the quarter is over will be paid up until today."

"I don't think that is a good idea," Elizabeth said quietly, her tone urgent.

Anne leveled a hard looking frown on Elizabeth before turning back to her housekeeper and steward. "Mr. Hayes is in my mother's . . . that is, my study, with a large strongbox that is locked inside the cabinet next to the door." She held out a key, which Mr. Greyson took. "Have him and it brought to the front parlor and request that everyone gather. I will see each of them in the parlor, one at a time."

Mr. Greyson appeared startled, but he bowed. "Yes, miss."

"Yes, miss," Mrs. Barclay echoed, curtsying again.

As soon as they left, Darcy watched Anne turn a glare on Elizabeth. "I would prefer you give me advice in private," Anne said stiffly. "I don't like you trying to undermine my authority."

"Is this sufficiently private?" Elizabeth asked, her tone contrite, though Darcy felt he knew her well enough to read anger in the set of her shoulders and jaw.

"Yes, it is."

Elizabeth took a quick breath. "Then let me tell you that if you do this, too many of the staff will leave. It wouldn't matter if only one or two went, but your mother was very generous with her bequests. You're going to lose more than a few."

Darcy hadn't thought of that, but once Elizabeth brought it to his attention, he shared her concern. The way Lady Catherine had constructed her will, all of the most experienced workers would be given enough that they could afford to leave if they wished. Those individuals were the ones needed most.

"I am not going back on my word," Anne said forcefully. "I'm sure the servants here are more loyal than you think, or are apparently accustomed to. They won't leave. Besides, they live here or nearby. Where would they go?"

Elizabeth turned beseeching eyes on Darcy, who cleared his throat, wondering if Anne was correct. His own staff was very loyal. He was certain of it.

"Darcy, come," Anne said, standing. "I want you by my side. You may certainly come too if you wish, Elizabeth, but please do not contradict me in front of the servants." With that, Anne marched from the room.

Darcy stood, surprised by Anne's forcefulness.

"Do you think I'm needed?" Mrs. Jenkinson asked.

"You should take some time for yourself," Elizabeth said before Darcy could answer. "I'll go."

Mrs. Jenkinson smiled, looking grateful, and began putting away her work.

Elizabeth rose, gathering up her sewing. "Shall we, Mr. Darcy?" she said, gesturing toward the door.

He nodded and turned to follow Anne. He wasn't sure if his cousin was doing the right thing, but thought her new attitude was a good sign. She would need a strong backbone to run Rosings. He just hoped they weren't helping her become another Lady Catherine.

They quickly caught up to Anne and the three of them paraded into the front parlor, where Mr. Hayes and the strongbox were waiting. He handed Anne the key she'd given Mr. Greyson and she used another key to open the strongbox.

The room was exceedingly formal, even the least expensive items of décor worth more than many men could hope to earn with years of labor. It was also dark, stuffy, garish, and Darcy's least favorite room in

Rosings.

Anne crossed to the stiff red settee boasting yards of golden fringe that was centered in the room. She settled herself on it, adjusted her shawl, and looked up at him and Elizabeth before turning to Mr. Hayes. "Please sit to my right, Mr. Hayes. I leave it to you to count out each amount correctly before passing it to me to bestow."

"Yes, miss," Mr. Hayes said, bobbing a bow. "A magnificent plan. A splendid idea."

Anne nodded as she turned back to Darcy. "Darcy, please sit to my left. Do your best to look as you normally do; aloof and imposing."

Darcy raised his eyebrows but crossed to take the indicated chair. It was outlandishly uncomfortable, something he knew from experience. The high back was so straight it seemed almost to lean inward into a man's spine, and the red and gold striped cushion was so stiff he'd often wondered if it was down-stuffed or simply covered-over wood.

Anne glanced at Elizabeth but didn't say anything.

Elizabeth said, "Do you want me to keep a record of who received how much money or would you prefer for Mr. Hayes to do it as he counts out the money?"

Anne's expression became uncertain. She looked from Elizabeth to Darcy.

"I was planning to do it," Mr. Hayes said, gesturing to an account book on the table.

"Seated where you are?" Darcy asked.

"I will stand up and make a note of it," Mr. Hayes said.

Everyone looked at Anne. "Arrange things so that they will be done more efficiently," she said, her tone once again commanding.

Darcy agreed with her choice. Although Mr. Hayes was being paid to help, there was no point in him standing up and sitting down for every servant. They rearranged the seating so that Darcy, Elizabeth, and Mr. Hayes sat at a large table with the account book and the strongbox on it. Mr. Hayes was seated closest to Anne so that he could hand her the bequests. Darcy was relieved that the chairs the servants brought were considerably more comfortable than the one Anne had first directed him to.

Once they were seated, Mr. Greyson stepped into the doorway. "Many of the servants are already here, miss. We've sent for the farm workers."

"Thank you, Greyson. Please begin showing them in. I'm sure the others will arrive before we're done."

"Yes, miss."

A line of maids and footmen began to file in. Mr. Greyson introduced each servant. Darcy read the amount from the account book and Mr. Hayes looked at it, saying, 'confirmed' with each amount. Elizabeth wrote the name of the person receiving the money on a receipt, giving it to Darcy to fill in the amount. Mr. Hayes then counted out the amount. Those who could sign the receipts did so. The others made their mark, which Darcy, Elizabeth, and Mr. Hayes witnessed.

As Anne handed out the bequests, Elizabeth would ask each beneficiary if they intended to stay. Most of them said they did not. Darcy could feel Anne growing more nervous as the afternoon wore on, a feeling he shared.

At one point, as Elizabeth handed him a receipt, her gaze met his. Darcy was struck by how bright her eyes were, his look lingering on hers. A beguiling flush brightened her cheeks. He wished that flush had something to do with him, but felt it rather more likely it had to do with her concern over the problem Anne was creating. After that silent exchange, if exchange it was, they both kept their eyes on the business at hand.

"A moment," Elizabeth said when the smiling cook entered.

The cook halted halfway across the room. "Miss?" she asked, casting a longing look at the money Mr. Hayes was counting out.

"You accepting this now is contingent upon cooking dinner tonight," Elizabeth said in a firm tone.

Darcy glanced at Anne, finding her regarding Elizabeth with wide eyes.

"Yes, miss," the cook said. "I've already done half the work."

"Fine," Elizabeth said. "Proceed."

The cook hurried forward, her smile reappearing, wider than before, as she accepted her sum.

If Anne looked distressed over how many of the household staff were leaving, Darcy was more than dismayed at the number of farm workers who said they would depart. True, more of them stayed than did members of the household staff, but there would be difficulty handling the stock and finishing the planting. He wondered how many of the fields hadn't been planted.

Finally, no one else seemed to be waiting without. Mr. Greyson and Mrs. Barclay entered.

"That is the last of them, miss," Mr. Greyson said. "Will you require anything else?"

"Not at this time, Greyson," Anne said, sounding tired. She looked smaller, as if the long afternoon of handing out Lady Catherine's bequests had diminished her.

"May we have our sums, then, miss?" Mrs. Barclay asked.

"Do you plan to stay?" Anne asked before Elizabeth had the opportunity.

"No, miss," Mrs. Barclay said. "With your lady mother's generosity, my husband and I can afford to retire. It's a blessing, it is. I thought we'd be working until the day we died, hardly ever to see one another. He works two villages over, you see. We only meet on our days off, if we can have them at the same time."

Darcy looked at the graying housekeeper, hoping his surprise didn't show on his face. How had he not known Mrs. Barclay had a husband? He wondered if his aunt had realized the woman wasn't widowed. As was the case at most estates, his housekeeper, Mrs. Reynolds, was a widow. He'd been fortunate to find a woman as capable as Mrs. Reynolds who didn't wish to remarry.

"I see," Anne said, handing Mrs. Barclay the money Hayes offered her. "Will you be staying, Greyson?"

"No, miss," Mr. Greyson said, his eyes on the sum Anne passed to him. "I've long dreamed of my own small dwelling, perhaps with a garden and some geese. A quiet place for my remaining years, near my grandchildren. My son has a cottage on his farm he's been begging me to take over since his last tenant left. Now I have enough money to do so without burdening him, thanks to Lady Catherine's generosity. I was always so very grateful to your mother for giving me a place of employment after my wife died. I never expected this additional gift."

"Well, I shall miss you both," Anne said, her voice weak.

"Thank you, Miss de Bourgh," Mrs. Barclay said. "It's been an honor serving you."

Clutching her money to her chest, Mrs. Barclay curtsied. Mr. Greyson bowed. They both hurried from the room. Anne sat stiff backed on the settee, looking stunned. Darcy felt a bit dumbfounded himself. A glance askance at Elizabeth, beside him, showed a wry smile barely visible on her downturned face.

Chapter Seven

Elizabeth dressed for dinner with a trepidation that was all too soon to be vindicated. The meal, which was quite plain, was served by a young, frazzled looking kitchen maid, as all of the footmen had left. With each sign of the maid's ineptitude, Anne's face became more drawn. Mr. Darcy looked grim, and Mrs. Jenkinson worried. There was little in the way of conversation, though Elizabeth suspected they were all thinking similarly.

Elizabeth knew it was on her and Mrs. Jenkinson to provide conversation. Mrs. Jenkinson seemed content to dine in silence, however, and Elizabeth wondered if she was no longer being paid and therefore no longer taking her role as companion to heart. For her part, Elizabeth found her place across from Mr. Darcy too disconcerting to allow for casual conversation. She kept picturing the look of astonishment on his face when he'd opened the door and seen her in her nightgown. She liked to think there'd been appreciation there as well, but schooled herself against such whimsical, pointless vanity.

She maintained hope that he was too much of a gentleman to be perusing similar thoughts and kept her eyes away from his face, making it difficult to speak to him. The last thing she wanted was to look up and catch his eyes on her, that intent look in them that she'd glimpsed in the parlor earlier that day. Something about that look had brought a blush to her cheeks and stolen her breath. She wasn't sure she cared for the sensation, especially not when it was caused by a man she was angry with for ruining Jane's happiness and for regarding her and her family with such complete disdain.

When the maid had cleared away the last course, Elizabeth stood. "I'm going to the kitchen to assess the situation," she said.

"Thank you," Anne said in a small voice.

Elizabeth made her way to the kitchen, only taking one wrong turn in the process. If Rosings weren't quite so large, she mused, it wouldn't require such a massive staff. Not that there was anything to do about the size of the place. She smiled, picturing Anne's face if she suggested they knock half the manor down. Her expression changed as the somber thought occurred to her that if they didn't find more servants they might have to close off a number of rooms.

Entering the kitchen, she found the cook and two maids clearing up. One of the maids was the girl who'd served them. She gave a startled squeak when Elizabeth walked in. The other maid and the cook exchanged glances.

"Thought we'd do the clearing up one last time," the cook said. She turned from the sink, wiping her hands on her apron. "I did the best I could with dinner, what with most everyone gone already."

"Dinner was fine," Elizabeth said. "Thank you for staying to prepare it."

"I hoped to stay the night, truth to tell, miss," the cook said. "It's a twenty mile walk to my kin and I didn't want to make it mostly in the dark. I plan to set out at daybreak."

"Tomorrow morning?" Elizabeth asked.

"Aye, miss, and I won't have time to be fixing no breakfast for anyone." The cook's face took on a mutinous cast. "I don't work here now."

Elizabeth nodded, smiling. She declined to point out that if the cook didn't want to work for Anne, she shouldn't expect a bed in Rosings that night. There was nothing to be gained by harassing the woman into preparing one more meal. They would have to learn to cope without her tomorrow, breakfast or not.

"I'm not very familiar with Kent," Elizabeth said. "Will you be safe walking twenty miles alone? If you leave early enough, I'm sure you can make it before dark."

"That's why I mean to go at first light," the cook said, relaxing at

Elizabeth's words. "We'll be well enough. I'm taking Jenny here with me and two of the farmhands that have folks out that way are traveling with us too." When she said Jenny, she gestured to the maid who hadn't served them. "We plan to rest every hour and we'll be bringing some bread. Sarah will be staying on with you, miss," she added, nodding toward the girl who had served them.

"I'm glad to hear you'll be safe," Elizabeth said, not commenting that they had no more right to take bread than they had to expect accommodations for the night. "I know you're busy clearing up, which is very kind of you, but would you mind giving me a few pointers for the morning? I don't know where anything is. I'm embarrassed to admit it, but I don't even know how to light the stove."

"I can show you where things are kept, miss," the cook said. "Sarah will be able to light the stove for you in the morning, but I can't tell you how to cook in an hour or two. The girls can finish clearing up."

Elizabeth walked about the kitchen with the cook, who gave her the key to the spice cabinet and pointed out the range of earthenware jars where various staples were kept. She took Elizabeth to the cold room where a ham hung and showed her the array of cured meats and root vegetables there, the latter greatly diminished as they neared the harvest season. There were shelves of preserved and dried fruits, roots and vegetables, kegs of beer and bottles of wine, which came with a second key.

"How old is Sarah?" Elizabeth asked as the tour wound down. They were in a room off of the kitchen, inspecting shelves stocked with preserves. Some of the jars looked old enough that Elizabeth wasn't sure the contents would still be edible.

"She's almost fifteen," the cook said. She gave Elizabeth a sympathetic look. "She'll work hard for you, miss. I'm sure it will all come out right."

"Thank you," Elizabeth said.

She didn't feel as optimistic as the cook sounded, but at least there was plenty of food. Now she needed to figure out how their stores would be turned into meals and served. She didn't fancy eating age-old preserves out of jars with spoons, although picturing Anne, Mrs. Jenkinson and the aloof Mr. Darcy seated about Lady Catherine's fancy dining table doing so restored her sense of humor.

"There are the animals as well, miss, to dine on, and chickens for eggs," the cook said, pulling Elizabeth from her musings.

Elizabeth nodded, at least somewhat familiar with that aspect of farming. Though on a much smaller scale, she'd grown up in a similar circumstance to how Rosings was run. "So we'll at least have fresh eggs in the morning," she said.

"And the bacon," the cook said. "Though you'll need to butcher another hog before long."

"I'll keep that in mind," Elizabeth said, vowing not to have anything to do with the actual butchering.

"Will that be all, then, miss?" the cook asked.

"Yes, thank you. You've been most instructive, and kind. Have a safe journey tomorrow."

The cook nodded and headed back into the kitchen. Elizabeth followed her out of the storeroom and left her inspecting Sarah's and Jenny's work. She made her way to Anne's favorite parlor, finding Mrs. Jenkinson and Anne both reading. Mr. Darcy stood at the window, a lean silhouette against the lowering sun. He leveled intent, serious eyes on her as she entered and Elizabeth had to fight down another blush.

"Well?" Anne asked, setting her book down. Elizabeth could see she was only a few pages into the volume and suspected Anne was too worried to read.

"The cook is leaving at first light. She has family about twenty miles from here and plans to walk. One of the maids is going with her as are two farm hands, so they will probably be safe. Only one kitchen maid will stay, but she's about fifteen and not very experienced."

"What do we do?" Anne asked, her eyes wide.

"Whatever we can. I would like to ask Mrs. Collins for help, if I may. She's quite capable. Mr. Darcy," Elizabeth said, lifting her gaze back to him. "I have no idea of what must be done for the farm and with the animals. Do you?"

"I believe so," he said turning fully from the window, his hands clasped behind his back. "Most important will be the daily care of the animals, which can't be allowed to falter, but we'll have a disaster if the crops aren't planted. I'll do what I can."

"Miss de Bourgh," Elizabeth said. "Does Mr. Darcy have your authority to hire people at more than the usual wage?"

Anne nodded, looking startled. Elizabeth wondered if she was surprised at the idea of paying more or at being asked. "Certainly."

"I'm going over to the parsonage to speak to Mrs. Collins," Elizabeth said. "We'll need her help first thing tomorrow if we and the remaining servants want to eat breakfast."

"I'll send for the carriage," Anne said.

"Who will you send?" Elizabeth asked with a slight smile. "I'll walk. I'm in want of exercise."

"Please allow me to escort you," Mr. Darcy said. "It will be dark before you return."

"Not if I leave promptly," Elizabeth said. "The parsonage grounds border Lady Catherine's and it's only half a mile."

He nodded, though he looked displeased. Elizabeth hurried from the room before anyone could object or see the color she could feel heating her cheeks. Did Mr. Darcy not realize he'd just suggested she walk alone with him, in the dark?

Chapter Eight

Elizabeth was pleased she woke quite early the following morning. She wanted to get down to the kitchen and see about breakfast before the rest of the household was up, although she was sure no one would expect the level of service they were accustomed to receiving at Rosings. She readied herself quickly, selecting her most worn gown as she didn't know what tasks lay ahead of her, and made her way to the kitchen.

She found Sarah already up and in the process of preparing the kitchen fire. "Good morning, Sarah."

"Good morning, miss," the girl said, looking up from her task.

"Are you comfortable doing that?" Elizabeth asked, unsure if the cook's assurance that Sarah could do so had been honest or meant to sooth.

"It's my usual job, miss," Sarah said. She straightened, using a towel to wipe soot off her hands.

"What can you cook?"

"Bread," Sarah said. She looked about the kitchen, her face taking on the same frantic cast it held the evening before when she'd served dinner. "I usually make the bread. Cook has arthritis in her hands and she didn't like to knead, so she taught me. Last night I boiled all the eggs and this morning I gave them out to those who lit out early, along with yesterday's bread. Cook told me to do that."

Elizabeth nodded, smiling to reassure the girl that she was doing well. She didn't begrudge the former servants having the food for their journeys, even though she'd had some uncharitable thoughts the previous evening.

"There'll be plenty more eggs for breakfast," Sarah said hurriedly.

She looked toward the door leading to the kitchen garden. "I just have to fetch them. I thought I'd start the water boiling for tea first, but I can get the eggs if you like."

"I can fetch the eggs," Elizabeth said. She crossed to the door where an empty basket rested. "I assume this is the basket?"

"Yes, miss."

"You stay here and work on the bread, which I can't do, and I'll take care of collecting what the chickens have given us. Mrs. Collins will be coming here soon. Please follow her advice."

"Yes, miss."

Elizabeth took the basket and headed out into the fresh morning air. Even more so than the evening before, she was pleased to be out of doors. She hadn't been at Rosings long, but she was feeling very stifled by the grand furnishings and plethora of ornate decorations. She was enjoying Anne's company well enough, but wished Miss de Bourgh showed some slight inclination to walk outside. Of course knowing Anne, she would walk so slowly it would drive Elizabeth mad, so perhaps things were better the way they were.

Elizabeth's long strides carried her across the grounds, past the kitchen garden and the stable, which were hidden from Rosings by a grove of fruit trees. She hadn't been to the henhouse, but she had no trouble finding it. She could hear the chickens as soon as she stepped outside. She could also hear someone working in the stable as she passed. She wondered if it was someone who'd stayed or if Mr. Darcy had somehow already managed to recruit people.

The henhouse was a bit larger than she'd expected, but she supposed Rosings was a great deal larger than homes she was accustomed to. Inside was just as full of clucking and squabbling chickens as any other coup Elizabeth had been in, the sunlight streaming in the doorway illuminating air full of floating bits of straw, dust moats and downy feathers. Not that she'd had much occasion to spend time in chicken coups, though her first time in one sprang swiftly to mind.

She'd wanted to talk to Charlotte in private and had followed her into the Lucas's coup to help her gather eggs. Elizabeth must have been about eleven at the time, making Charlotte eighteen. Elizabeth considered that the beginning of their friendship, their whispered words and shared giggles inside the chicken coup. It was odd, but she couldn't remember what had seemed so important for her to talk to Charlotte about. She did remember Charlotte telling her not to say anything to Mrs. Bennet about gathering eggs, a task Elizabeth's mother would consider beneath her.

As she stuck her hands under the chickens now, filling her basket, she was glad Charlotte had taught her to collect eggs that day. If only she'd paid more attention to Charlotte's practical lessons, she wouldn't feel so helpless in the kitchen. Fortunately, her friend was near enough to teach her now.

Elizabeth stepped out of the coup with a full basket, closing the door behind her. She frowned, considering her own thoughts. If Charlotte's practical lessons were so useful, should Elizabeth revisit her friend's most adamant one, that marriage was for pragmatic reasons, not sentimental ones?

Elizabeth shook her head, setting off across the grounds. What did it matter if Charlotte was right about that as well? It wasn't as if anyone waited to propose to Elizabeth now, of practical worth or not.

Walking back toward the manor, Elizabeth realized she could see into the stable from the side the coup was on. For all the activity she'd heard on the way past before, there appeared to be only one man working. He was excessively tall and well built, with dark breeches and rolled up shirtsleeves. She wondered who he was, for he certainly didn't look like a typical farm hand. He paused in his work, leaning on the pitchfork he was using, and glanced over his shoulder.

"Mr. Darcy," Elizabeth exclaimed, shocked.

He turned to face her, moving the pitchfork to one hand so he could bow. "Miss Bennet. A pleasant morning to you."

Elizabeth realized she'd stopped walking and hurriedly resumed, closing the distance between them. She hoped he hadn't noticed her utter shock at his appearance. "Forgive me for not curtsying," she said. "The basket makes it awkward."

"Forgive me for my state of disarray," he said.

He nodded toward the back of the barn and she realized his coat hung there, his cravat dangling from the collar. Her eyes dropped to the skin exposed at his neck and she quickly looked away. "I shouldn't keep you from working," she said, willing herself not to blush.

How he evoked such a rush of heat to her face she didn't understand. No other man ever had. Not even Wickham, back when she'd thought she might possibly fall in love with him. She didn't even care for Mr. Darcy, she reminded herself, though she did respect him. She also owed him an apology for misjudging him, but wasn't sure how to begin it.

"I was looking for an excuse to stop working for a few moments and couldn't have asked for a better one," Mr. Darcy said.

Elizabeth looked up, surprised by what sounded almost like flattery. She scanned the yard, searching for something to say. "The farm workers can't all have left. Is there no other to take on this task? Mucking out the stalls seems particularly onerous."

He shrugged. "No, all of the workers haven't left. Those who remain are far better than I am at various tasks that can't be left undone. The only two who are as unskilled as I am are a ten-year-old boy and his grandfather. Tending the horses requires no special skill, only strength, which neither of them has in abundance."

Unspoken was the fact that he was more than strong enough for the task. "Will you be able to hire people?" she asked, wondering why it felt as if there wasn't quite enough air in her lungs for speaking.

"Yes, by paying double the usual wage," he said.

"Double?" Elizabeth was shocked. She'd known he would need to pay above the normal wage, but double seemed extreme.

"It's necessary. People are leaving farms for factories. Too many men are fighting Napoleon."

"Too many or not enough?"

"You don't agree we're spread too thin?" Darcy said, smiling slightly. "It can be argued that we should give up some of our farther holdings and consolidate against Bonaparte."

"It can also be argued that we should cultivate more allies," Elizabeth said, playing the foil. "Why should England relinquish any more than she already has?"

"You're an imperialist," Darcy said.

"I am simply suggesting that England is strong," Elizabeth replied. She turned her face more fully into the morning sun, returning his smile. It was invigorating to be out of doors and to be having a real discussion about a relevant topic, not stitching away in a stuffy parlor while debating which of Lady Catherine's gowns were salvageable.

"England is strong," Darcy agreed, looking down at her in that intent way of his. "As is Rosings, I hope. How is the household managing?"

"We won't starve," she said, displaying her basket of chicken eggs. "Though I doubt we'll want eggs for every meal. I now wish I'd helped in the kitchen at home. I know nothing about what to do. I'm glad Mrs. Collins will be able to teach me."

"You shouldn't have to learn," Darcy said. "I'm a bit surprised Mrs. Collins knows so much."

"She has always been very dedicated to being useful," Elizabeth said. In truth, Charlotte had worried she would never marry and thus have to stay to help her parents and then, hopefully, brother. "She won't be able to help us every day, though. She has her own household. I will have to learn."

"There are agencies in London where servants can be hired," he said. He reached out, his fingers hovering over her hands where they held the basket. "These hands are for stitching and playing the pianoforte, not for turning red and callused with kitchen chores."

"These hands have had more than their fill of stitching lately, thank you, and gathering eggs certainly won't harm them. Not unless the hens take particular exception to me."

"How could they possibly contrive that?" he asked.

Elizabeth cleared her throat, the feeling that she couldn't quite breathe well enough returning. "We won't have to find out if you can arrange for servants to be sent here from London," she said. "What will it take?"

"Money," he said, dropping his hand. "And Miss de Bourgh has plenty. I can have servants hired. I have an agent in London who can see to it. The most important thing is to handle the stock and get the planting done, and London servants won't help with that."

He looked over his shoulder at the stable and Elizabeth realized he was about to return to his task. She would miss her chance to apologize. She'd hoped for the conversation to somehow come around to it more smoothly, but she would have to do her best regardless.

"Mr. Darcy," she said before he could take his leave. "I want to apologize for misjudging you so badly. I was a fool to believe Mr. Wickham."

His face took on such a grim cast that she wished she hadn't spoken. "Many others have been fooled by him, including my father."

"The clues were there, if I'd only looked for them. Really, I feel a terrible fool and I treated you unjustly in that regard."

"Only in that regard?" he said, his eyes narrowing. She opened her mouth to speak but he held up his hand, staying her. "No, you are correct. In some regards I am at fault. You have two apologies due from me," he said. "The first is for my trying to enter your room when I returned to Rosings. In the past, I have had the use of that room."

"That makes it perfectly understandable and it was clearly an accident," Elizabeth said, unable to suppress a blush this time. "Your apology is accepted."

"Thank you for understanding," he said.

"I do, and I recommend we don't speak of it again," Elizabeth said. "What, may I ask, is the second apology for?" She could think of two grievances she harbored against him, not one.

80

"The second is for insulting your family when I proposed to you and in my letter. There was no need for that. I was unthinking when I proposed and bitter and angry when I wrote the letter."

So he still felt no remorse for separating Jane from the man she loved. Elizabeth endeavored to be civil. He was apologizing, after all. "Your anger was understandable, since I was rude. The letter, perhaps, began in bitterness, but it did not end so. The adieu is charity itself."

He nodded, looking relieved. Elizabeth was pleased he'd thought to apologize for his insults, but in spite of her reply, she wasn't completely satisfied on that score. He'd apologized for voicing his insults, but hadn't said that he didn't still believe them. Nor did he seem to care one whit about Bingley and Jane.

Nevertheless, she felt more sympathetic toward him than she ever had before. She supposed that seeing a different side of Mr. Darcy had something to do with it. She saw a man who was willing to shed his privileged identity when work needed to be done. Before this morning, she would never have imagined Mr. Darcy would condescend to work in a stable.

Once again, Elizabeth took in his state of half-dress, without his coat. His dark hair was in disarray and exertion had brought life to his visage. He was no longer cold, aloof and reserved, but rather vital and animated. She looked down at her own bedraggled appearance, acutely conscious of her flyaway hair, the basket she held between them and her utilitarian clothing.

Desirous of looking anywhere but back into Mr. Darcy's intense gaze, Elizabeth scanned the roadway. It took her a moment to realize she saw a rider coming toward them. As he drew nearer, she recognized someone she'd seen in church. He was perhaps twenty-five and had fair hair and cheerful blue eyes. It soon became apparent that he was headed toward them. He brought his horse to a halt nearby and swung down from the saddle with practiced ease.

"Mr. Darcy," he said, bowing.

"Mr. Whitaker," Mr. Darcy said, returning the greeting. "Miss

Bennet, may I introduce Mr. Whitaker?"

"Miss Bennet," Mr. Whitaker said, bowing to her with a friendly and, she thought she imagined, appreciative smile.

Elizabeth made a slight curtsy, doing the best she could not to cover her hem in farmyard dust. "Mr. Whitaker."

"Mr. Darcy," Mr. Whitaker said, though he was still looking at her. "I've heard about your problems with your servants."

Elizabeth raised her eyebrows. "News travels quickly here, I see."

"My property abuts Rosings to the south," Mr. Whitaker said. "Some of Rosings former servants passed through last night." He turned to Mr. Darcy. "I have two experienced farm workers you could borrow for two weeks, if you wish."

"That would be greatly appreciated," Mr. Darcy said, though he'd returned to his usual withdrawn self, his face no longer open or his tone easy. "We'll pay them double, but tell them they must return to you. We need people to look after the stock."

"One of the maids was raised on a farm and could help with the milking," Elizabeth said. Mr. Darcy and Mr. Whitaker both turned to her in surprise. "I asked last night when I returned from the parsonage," she said, amused at their reaction. Did they feel that once greetings had been exchanged and her person admired there was no further place for her in the conversation, or did they assume she knew nothing of how a farm worked? She'd been raised on a farm and knew the importance of milking.

"That would help, thank you," Mr. Darcy said.

"Milking and feeding are the two most important things to see you're getting done," Mr. Whitaker said.

"I think we have them about in hand, though Miss Bennet finding a maid to help with the milking will make things easier. It will free up a farmhand for planting. It's the planting I'm concerned about," Mr. Darcy said.

"Aye, you won't have any feed to give them, or you and the rest of Rosings, if the planting doesn't get done. Weather's holding well, too,"

Mr. Whitaker said. "Would be a shame not to get seed in the ground before the next bout of rain hits."

"Any notion of how long it will hold off?" Mr. Darcy said, frowning.

"If you'll excuse me," Elizabeth said. "I need to take these to the kitchen or breakfast will be sparse." As much as she enjoyed sparing with Mr. Darcy on various issues, she'd heard farmers make predictions about the weather all of her life, and never known any to be particularly accurate or very interesting.

"Miss Bennet," Mr. Darcy said, bowing to her.

"Miss Bennet," Mr. Whitaker echoed.

Elizabeth made her way back across the yard. The morning was so fair, she briefly regretted making her excuses. It would be worth listening to men speak earnestly about the weather to stay out of doors. She knew there was much to do indoors, though, so she hurried inside to help with breakfast.

A warm, light-filled kitchen smelling of bacon and bread greeted her. Elizabeth stopped, taking in the well-ordered chaos. Sarah was still there, along with two maids Elizabeth recognized from the parsonage, Charlotte's sister Maria, and Charlotte herself. She looked over from where she stood skimming cream, offering Elizabeth a smile.

"Charlotte," Elizabeth exclaimed, stepping into the kitchen. "I am so pleased to find you here. You have my unending gratitude."

"Good morning, Elizabeth," Charlotte said. "I'm not sure you'll agree after I've made you work all morning, but it can't be helped. I can't remain here all day so I intend to set you on the right path for breakfast, luncheon and dinner."

Elizabeth laughed, an enthusiasm which carried her through the morning. Charlotte hadn't been exaggerating when she said they would work, but Elizabeth found the work enjoyable. She could finally see the appeal it held for her friend. There was a certain feeling of empowerment that went with learning how to actually do things. Simmering sauces and slicing bread was a good deal more fun than spending endless hours stitching seams into black garments. At least in the kitchen one moved about.

She worked through breakfast, eating several slices of fresh buttered bread, and they moved on to setting luncheon and dinner into motion. Elizabeth had never before appreciated how much work went into the meals that came from a gentrified kitchen each day, though she was aware Charlotte had them preparing a simpler fare than was typical. She finished her tasks for the morning with a heightened respect for cooks everywhere.

"I must return to the parsonage," Charlotte said as the cleared up. "Sarah, will you be able to see to lunch?"

"Yes ma'am," Sarah said from where she was scrubbing cookware.

"I can keep helping," Elizabeth said.

Charlotte gave her a little shake of her head. "I'm sure Sarah will be quite able to cope, now that everything is set in motion. The roast we put in will likely last for days, and the vegetables can be served again before the remainder are turned into soup." She smiled about the kitchen, turning her gaze on the two kitchen maids she'd brought with her. "Come back as soon as you've finished helping Sarah with lunch. Walk me out, please, Elizabeth?"

Elizabeth nodded, untying the apron she'd donned earlier at Charlotte's insistence. She hung it where she'd found it and turned toward the doorway leading to the front hall, but Charlotte crossed to the kitchen door and let herself out. Elizabeth followed her into the sunshine, enjoying the warmth of it on her face. Charlotte walked a few paces away from the kitchen, then turned to Elizabeth with serious eyes.

"What we did today was necessary and irreproachable," Charlotte said.

"Of course it was," Elizabeth said, surprised by her friend's choice of topic.

"And will also be the end of you helping in the kitchen."

"Was I truly that poor of a cook?" Elizabeth asked, amused.

"You are to be no sort of cook at all, Lizzy," Charlotte said, frowning. "You don't see the risk here, do you? You must maintain the dignity of your station. Your place in this household will afford you the chance to meet any number of eligible gentlemen. They can't see you as hired help, nor can you permit the staff to. You'll never make a good match if you're known to practice labor."

Elizabeth let out a sigh, wishing that a young lady's energies didn't have to be devoted to that all-important match that would move her from her father's household into the security of being a wedded woman. "I enjoyed cooking."

"I only want to see you settled as advantageously as you can be," Charlotte said. "Promise me you won't do any more menial tasks?"

After spending the morning learning what went into preparing edible food, Elizabeth wasn't sure cooking qualified as menial, but she nodded. While she didn't long for matrimony, Elizabeth knew it would be her lot in life and she'd need to make the best of that. A man like Mr. Darcy wouldn't wed a miss with water-reddened hands and flour in her hair. Yet if she didn't do it, who would? "I can't. Things need to be done."

"Only for a week then, and never for more than half a day. After a week, you will become a lady again."

"That is reasonable."

"Thank you," Charlotte said. "I'll walk myself home. Go enjoy the luncheon you labored over."

"Thank you for your assistance," Elizabeth said. She hoped Charlotte knew she meant the advice as well as the practical skills. Charlotte was an older sister in ways Jane never could be. Too trusting and naive, Jane often seemed younger than she was. Elizabeth was the one who fell into the role of protector.

They exchanged a quick hug and parted ways. Elizabeth returned through the kitchen, smiling at the still working maids. Seeing she wasn't needed, she hurried to her room to reorder her appearance and then went down to dine with Anne and Mrs. Jenkinson, who were waiting for her. Elizabeth took in the three lonely place settings with no

85

spot laid for Mr. Darcy at the foot of the table, but made sure her pleasant expression didn't waver. It would have been a more interesting meal if Mr. Darcy would have joined them.

As it was, it was not a stimulating meal. The food was perfectly acceptable but limited by the skills and resources at hand. What little conversation there was revolved around Anne's wardrobe. Elizabeth found herself hardly able to attend to what was said and contributing little.

"They tell me you worked in the kitchen all morning," Anne said. "Elizabeth?"

"Yes?" Elizabeth blinked, realizing Anne had been speaking to her. She ran her mind over what had just been said. "That is, yes, I was. I also gathered eggs."

"It must have been exhausting," Anne said. "I can understand why you'd be tired now."

Elizabeth shrugged, grateful Anne had interpreted her quiet as fatigue. "It was an unfamiliar way to spend a morning."

"Do you think you're well enough to help me with some letters?" Anne asked.

"Undoubtedly," Elizabeth replied. Glancing at Anne's plate, Elizabeth could see she hadn't eaten much. She toyed with a piece of bread, breaking it into little pieces. Elizabeth supposed the food wasn't really up to Anne's standards.

As soon as the interminable meal was over, they retired to Anne's favorite study, where she directed Elizabeth to the writing desk. Giving Elizabeth only a vague sense of content, Anne went over what letters should be written. Elizabeth at first assumed she would write them for Anne to sign, but Anne asked her to start each letter by saying she was writing on behalf of Miss de Bourgh and to sign her own name. She then left Elizabeth to it, sitting on the sofa to read while Mrs. Jenkinson sewed nearby.

Elizabeth was nearly done with the final letter, finding her back stiff from the task, when a harried looking maid hurried in. "A Mrs. Allen, ma'am," the maid said, not even remaining long enough for the plump woman to enter the room.

Mrs. Allen gazed after the retreating servant with a bemused look before crossing the room and dipping a curtsy to Anne. "Anne, it's lovely to see you, though I am sorry for the circumstances."

Elizabeth paused in her work to study Anne's cousin. From Anne's description of her, Elizabeth had expected Mrs. Allen to be both lazy and heavy. She was a little plump, but not seriously so. Her eyes held a liveliness Elizabeth usually associated with intelligence.

"Penny," Anne said. She lowered her book, but didn't close it. "It's so good of you to come. I'm afraid things aren't progressing as I could have hoped." Anne gestured limply toward where Elizabeth sat at the desk, across the room. "You recall my companion, Mrs. Jenkinson and that is my friend Miss Bennet, who has kindly agreed to stay with me until the situation I find myself in is sorted. Elizabeth, this is my cousin, Mrs. Penelope Allen."

Mrs. Jenkinson and Mrs. Allen exchanged nods of greeting. Elizabeth set aside her pen. She stood and curtsied, a gesture Mrs. Allen returned. Elizabeth crossed the room to join them as Mrs. Allen turned back to Anne.

"What situation is that, cousin?" Mrs. Allen asked.

"I'm afraid I've all but ruined Rosings in a matter of days," Anne said, sounding miserable.

Elizabeth raised her eyebrows. "That is an exceptionally untrue statement," she said. "You have done no such thing, Miss de Bourgh. I'll own that we are having some difficulty with the staff, but nothing irreparable." She turned to address Mrs. Allen. "Lady Catherine was exceedingly generous in her bequeaths. Many of the more experienced household and farm staff have taken the opportunity to retire, as is their right."

"I see," Mrs. Allen said. She looked about the room. "Where would you say the most pressing need is? Within the house, of course. I know nothing of farming." She smiled, her hazel eyes twinkling.

Elizabeth felt she liked Mrs. Allen already. "The kitchen. The cook left and all of the kitchen maids save one. Linens and dusting can wait, but food simply cannot. The parson's wife was good enough to spend the morning here helping with breakfast and luncheon, but she has her own household to manage. She set dinner in motion in so much as she could, before she left."

"How fortuitous," Mrs. Allen said. "For I am quite familiar with what goes on in a kitchen. I'll go settle my things and get straight to assessing the likelihood of dinner."

Elizabeth looked to Anne, but Miss de Bourgh was gazing distractedly at a spot over Mrs. Allen's shoulder. "Thank you," Elizabeth said, realizing Anne wouldn't speak. "It would be very much appreciated."

Mrs. Allen nodded, dropped a curtsy and hurried away. Elizabeth turned to Anne, noting her pallor. "Are you well?"

"I'm tired. I think I will go to my room," Anne said. "Will you finish the letters and leave them on the desk? I'll see that they are posted."

"I will. Could we speak on what must be done to address the staffing issue before you retire?"

Anne frowned. "I'm sure you will do whatever needs to be done."

"It really isn't my place," Elizabeth said. She couldn't be making decisions about the running of Rosings. She was a guest and had no connection to the family at all. "Perhaps Mrs. Allen--"

Anne interrupted her with a shake of her head. "You're the one who realized the mistake I was making with the servants. You're the one I trust. You and Darcy. You both have my permission to make any decisions needed to repair the damage I've done."

"It was an understandable error," Elizabeth said. "You couldn't have known how the servants would react."

"You did," Anne said, looking down. "I asked you to remain here to guide me away from grievous errors, and the first time I disagreed with you, I ignored you." She raised stricken eyes to Elizabeth. "What if I am never prepared to manage Rosings?"

"Nothing truly disastrous has happened," Elizabeth said firmly. "We'll put this to right. Soon Rosings will be running so smoothly, you'll hardly need to concern yourself with it. All will be well. I wouldn't condescend to placate you."

Anne sighed, nodding. She passed a trembling hand across her face. "I must rest," she said. "Please see that I am not disturbed." Taking her book with her, she left the room.

Elizabeth stared after her, concerned. She knew Anne was of frail health, but had thought much of that had been prevarication to avoid her mother. Now Elizabeth was forced to wonder how serious Anne's infirmity was. Her worrying was interrupted as a maid hurried into the room, looking about, though obviously not for Elizabeth.

"May I help you?" Elizabeth asked.

"There are two women to see Miss de Bourgh," the girl said. "They say they would like to work here. Do you know where she's gone to, miss?"

"I do," Elizabeth said. "She's retired to her room and does not wish to be disturbed."

"What should I tell them?" the maid asked, wringing her hands.

"Show them into the front parlor," Elizabeth said. "Please ask Mrs. Allen to join me there. We shall speak with them."

The maid nodded and hurried away.

Elizabeth turned to look at Mrs. Jenkinson, realizing she was carefully folding her sewing. "Will you assist me in interviewing the women?"

Mrs. Jenkinson gave her a small smile. "I will not. I am sorry, Elizabeth, but Mrs. Allen's arrival is my opportunity to depart. Miss de Bourgh already released me from her service. I've remained for propriety's sake, hers and yours."

"You're leaving this moment?" Elizabeth asked, feeling bereft.

"Almost. It will take me a few minutes to finish packing and then I will go join my travel companions. I've already made arrangements. A young man who worked on the farm and his wife have been holding off on leaving to wait for me. I've offered them a small sum to take me with them in their wagon. They're headed toward my sister's home."

"I'm sorry to see you leave," Elizabeth said, though she could understand it. It was sad how Lady Catherine's interference had taken the woman who should have been Anne's closest friend and made her almost an enemy. "Will you say goodbye to Miss de Bourgh?"

"I will. Good luck here, Miss Bennet. She's fortunate to have you."

"Thank you. Safe travels."

Mrs. Jenkinson nodded. Elizabeth watched her return to putting away her sewing and then hurried from the room. She took a deep breath as she headed toward the front parlor, hoping she was up to the task she'd given herself. If Anne, who had lived there her whole life, couldn't manage Rosings, what hope had Elizabeth of doing so?

The first two women to arrive were by no means the last. All afternoon, all manner of people showed up. It was obvious that word had gotten out quickly. Elizabeth and Mrs. Allen met with each candidate. Elizabeth had no idea how to conduct such interviews, but she ended up doing so. Mrs. Allen chose to sit to the side, not asking questions. She was, however, surprisingly adamant on whom to hire. Fortunately, Elizabeth agreed with her choices. By evening, they had enough staff to keep things going, although not nearly with the level of service to which Anne was accustomed.

Chapter Nine

Darcy looked down at himself as he crossed the yard in the late afternoon light and elected to take the servants' corridors to his room. Arriving there, he was pleased to see his valet Stevens and the majority of his possessions had finally caught up with him. Especially given the state his shirt, trousers and boots were in.

"Sir," Stevens greeted, bowing.

"How is the little one?" Darcy asked.

"Thriving, sir."

"Glad to hear it."

Stevens wrinkled his nose, but didn't say anything as he assisted Darcy from his coat. "Miss Bennet arranged for you to have hot water for your bath."

"That was considerate of her," Darcy said, grateful and a bit surprised she'd thought of him. After a day which combined physical labor with decisions on what could be neglected and what had to be done, he was looking forward to soaking in a tub. He was also hungry in spite of his midday meal with the laborers.

"Indeed," Stevens agreed. He left Darcy to bathe, holding his boots and clothing out at arm's length as he carried them away.

Later, clean and decently clothed, Darcy came down to the parlor to find three women sewing, though not the precise three he'd expected. Mrs. Jenkinson appeared to have been replaced. The new addition to the seemingly endless task was a mature, rounded woman Darcy recognized as a much older than recalled version of Anne's cousin. He'd met Mrs. Allen only a few times in his life, and not seen her in many years, but she was recognizable enough.

"Anne, Mrs. Allen, Miss Bennet," Darcy greeted, bowing to them.

He wondered where Mrs. Jenkinson was.

"Mr. Darcy," Mrs. Allen said, jumping up. She set her sewing aside and crossed to curtsy before him. "Why, you've matured since last we met."

Darcy nodded. His eyes strayed to Elizabeth, her smile visible even though her face was cast toward her work. "You look well," he said.

"Thank you," Mrs. Allen said. "I do believe that with your arrival, we may partake of dinner at last."

"Will Mrs. Jenkinson be joining us?" he asked.

Anne sighed.

"She left," Elizabeth said.

"But we won't allow that to spoil our dinner," Mrs. Allen said with a smile.

"Of course not," Elizabeth said. "We knew she planned to go."

Darcy offered Mrs. Allen his arm. "I hope the meal is acceptable to you, Mrs. Allen. You are aware, I'm sure, of our circumstances." Mrs. Allen settled her fingers lightly on his forearm and he steered them toward dinner, wishing it was Elizabeth he was escorting, even for so short a walk.

"Oh, dinner promises to be lovely," Mrs. Allen said. "So many of the families sent over food this afternoon, I don't know what we shall do with it all."

"Splendid," Darcy said.

When they reached the dining room, he could see there were no footmen. With a bow, he left Mrs. Allen's side and moved to pull out Anne's chair for her. Anne looked somehow too weak to move the heavy piece of furniture at the head of the table herself. She was also too pale. He hoped enough care was being taken of his frail cousin.

Anne seated, Darcy eyed the place settings in momentary confusion. All of them were clustered about the head of the table, though normally he would have been seated at the foot. Were the few remaining servants truly that untrained?

"I asked them to set it this way," Anne said in a low voice.

Darcy looked down to see her watching him.

"There are so few of us and we're all good friends," Anne said. "I don't like the idea of everyone spaced out about this too long table, unable to speak without raising our voices. My mother could speak loud enough to be heard anywhere in the room, but I cannot. Please, sit beside me, Darcy." She gestured to her right. "Elizabeth, I would like you to sit here," Anne added, pointing to the seat across from his. A footman moved forward to help.

As he seated himself, Darcy hardly noticed that Mrs. Allen sat to his right, since he was far more interested in Elizabeth opposite him. Her skin had a beatific glow he could only accredit to an active day and fine constitution. As their first course was served, he searched his mind for some topic on which to engage her.

"Did your day go well, Mr. Darcy?" Elizabeth asked.

"Well enough. Mr. Whitaker's loan of farm hands was quite welcome."

"He sent food as well," Elizabeth said. She then rattled off the names of five other families who'd sent food. "According to what I've been able to learn, all of them have eligible men in them."

Darcy glanced at Anne, who pushed her food about on her plate. Though he and Elizabeth sat on either side of her, Anne didn't seem to be attending to the conversation. His worry for her deepened. She was obviously in no state to begin receiving the barrage of suitors that would wish to come. He was glad she was refusing visitors, but that shouldn't last indefinitely.

At his pause, Elizabeth turned politely to engage Mrs. Allen, leaving Darcy to attempt to engage his cousin. Overall, it proved to be a pleasant dinner, though Darcy preferred the private conversation he and Elizabeth had engaged in earlier that day. It hadn't been private enough, as they'd been interrupted, but he knew it was the most he could hope for.

The following morning, after having observed Anne all evening, Darcy was unsurprised she was ill. He was also unsurprised that Stevens had found some less fine garments for him to wear out to the fields. Pressing his worry for Anne away, aware that Elizabeth would care for her, Darcy dressed in the slightly coarse fabric. The style was outdated, and he could only assume they were some of his late uncle's clothes, likely reserved for similar activities. As Darcy recalled from boyhood, his uncle enjoyed the out-of-doors and often assisted on the farm, much to his wife's chagrin.

Over the next few days, life settled into a manageable routine. Darcy spent most of his waking hours ensuring the farmstead didn't falter. He wrote to his man in London, asking for an experienced housekeeper to be sent, but was too occupied to do any more to assist in that matter. That the household was running at all with the still limited, inexperienced and new staff was a minor miracle, which Darcy mostly accredited to Elizabeth. After neighboring families realized that bringing food to Miss de Bourgh would not get their unmarried sons a chance to court her, that source dried up, but between them, Elizabeth and Mrs. Allen managed.

Miss Kitty Bennet arrived, filling their meals with greater chatter. Darcy had all but forgotten Anne sending for the girl and at first wished she hadn't, for his cousin remained ill. He worried that Kitty Bennet, with her silliness and loquaciousness, would add too much additional burden on the other women. Instead, she took to reading to Anne, which seemed to actually comfort his indisposed cousin.

When the housekeeper he'd sent for arrived from London, Darcy hoped she would alleviate the remaining problems in the household, but she was sent back after a few days as it was discovered she was too fond of wine. Even without her, things continued to slowly improve. Darcy could tell Elizabeth was gaining experience in the role Anne had thrust her into. Every night, he gave a brief description of his day's activities and listened to the women tell him about theirs.

Generally, Mrs. Allen spoke only of managing the kitchen. Anne ceased attending their meals, staying in bed. She developed a cough and a fever, which worried him, but he knew she was being cared for and that she often had these bouts of illness. Surely she would recover this time, as always before.

Miss Kitty, to Darcy's surprise, took to speaking of the books she was reading to his cousin. Reading seemed to be broadening her mind, also to his surprise. He wouldn't have guessed she had a mind to be broadened. Then, she was related to Elizabeth, who was undeniably intelligent.

Elizabeth was also unfailingly cheerful, in spite of all the setbacks at getting Rosings running properly. She was lively, but sublimely decorous. She was teaching herself to manage a household the size of Rosings with little guidance, yet at an admirable pace. She was also beguiling as she sat across from him each evening, her dark hair shimmering in the light of the candles and her bow shaped lips unfailingly turned up at the corners. In short, she was perfection.

Which was why Darcy was glad she took to collecting the chicken eggs every morning. He made sure he was always working nearby so he could see her. She usually stopped to chat briefly. When they received the news that the Prime Minister, Spencer Perceval, had been assassinated, they had a lot to talk about. They speculated about possible political reasons for the assassination. Though it turned out to simply be a man who had a private grievance against the government, Darcy was happy to talk about such an important event with someone who was aware of the political situation.

Not that he was entirely without male company. Mr. Whitaker came over every few days and assisted, seemingly willing to do any needed task. He helped supervise workers, oversaw the planting of some of the fields, and even groomed horses alongside Darcy's coachman, Alderson. Darcy became quite impressed with the man, the only one of the neighbors who had done so much for them, especially after most realized Anne was not yet ready to be courted.

As when the servants first left, Darcy continued to do a lot of the physical work. He maintained his position that this was to free up more skilled workers for their tasks, but it was also so that he could fall in bed exhausted each night. Exhaustion represented his only chance to find sleep. Elizabeth's friendliness was causing him to want her all the more. Thoughts of her, especially the particularly beguiling notion of her beside his bed in her nightgown but with him in it waiting for her instead of standing in the doorway, were driving him mad.

He knew he shouldn't let her friendliness fool him. Elizabeth was routinely cordial to everyone, sometimes enough so to make him jealous of other men, like Mr. Whitaker. Her behavior was only natural. Logically they should try to get along. They all had to work together to solve Rosings' problems. Elizabeth had made it very clear she didn't like him. Her friendly greetings were no more than a combination of a cheerful disposition and a common sense reaction to their situation. Perhaps there was a little guilt thrown in for having misjudged him, but that didn't mean she saw him in the same light in which he saw her.

The trouble was, he hadn't stopped loving her and logic had little place in his mind in the deep of the night. Once, he found himself getting out of bed with the half-asleep thought that he should go to her. He lay back down, glad he didn't sleepwalk. He knew he must stop thinking of Elizabeth in that way, but the gap between knowing and doing seemed too wide for his heart to breach.

He thought that after Elizabeth's angry refusal of his proposal he would do what she wanted him to do: Convince himself that his offer was a mistake and be grateful she'd refused him. Instead, he found himself more deeply entranced with every passing day. More worrying, his fascination wasn't just with her beguiling physical attributes, but with her wit. Why, with little training or background, she was learning how to manage Rosings, and under trying circumstances. What a mistress of Pemberley she would make!

He was also managing his side of things well. In fact, Rosings' properties were running smoothly enough that he began to have a hard time coming up with excuses for being in the right place to meet Elizabeth in the mornings. Sometimes of late, all he achieved was a friendly wave. On those mornings, he told himself that he ate dinner with her every evening and that should be enough, but it wasn't.

Realizing he was extending his own suffering, Darcy resolved that things must change. Rosings would be in a state to allow him to leave soon, especially if Richard could be persuaded to return. In truth, Darcy had his own holdings to see to. He couldn't remain in Kent with Elizabeth forever. He resolved that the next time she stopped and spoke with him would be the last day he'd arrange himself to meet her. It had to be so, or he'd lose what was left of his tortured heart.

The following morning, making little pretense at work, he stood outside the stable, knowing it was the path she would take. Looking toward the manor, he peered through the fruit trees. He saw the kitchen door open and Elizabeth step out. The morning sun gave her dark hair a hint of red. He knew she was graceful in a ballroom, but watching her walk over uneven ground with a soft breeze blowing each errant curl was intoxicating. Sometimes, the wind blew her clothing against her slender form, revealing the outline of her body. It was much more provocative than seeing her in her nightgown, though he treasured that image for the intimacy of it.

She reached him more quickly than he would have hoped, as he wanted to savor their last meeting. "Miss Bennet," he said, bowing.

"Mr. Darcy," she replied as she dipped a curtsy, something she'd now mastered doing while burdened with a basket.

"I noticed we've been serving fewer eggs of late. Are the hens not laying well?" Darcy had no desire to speak to Elizabeth of chickens, but his brain was strangely blank as the anguished thought of leaving Rosings filled him.

"I've let a few of the hens keep their eggs. The new cook used three for soup for Miss de Bourgh and eventually there will need to be replacement hens."

"I'm glad she is eating," Darcy said.

"She's still feverish, but I think she's getting better. Does she get sick like this often?"

"Three or four times a year, I believe." He also didn't really want to speak to Elizabeth of his cousin either, though he was pleased she was improving.

"I wanted to leave by now, but I feel I can't when she is so ill."

Darcy didn't want her to leave, at least not until he forced himself to, but felt compelled to say, "She will be cared for."

She shook her head, not looking convinced. "Mrs. Allen does a good job of seeing that the kitchen is well run, but she pays little attention to Anne and no attention to the overall running of Rosings. We can't replace all of the people who left Rosings like hens. I'm still collecting eggs because we don't yet have enough people."

She blushed beguilingly as she said it, though Darcy couldn't imagine why. He forced himself to catch up with the conversation at hand, pulling his gaze from her lips. "More can be hired. I can send to London. What is needed?"

"Why don't I discuss it with everyone and talk to you tomorrow?"

He nodded.

"Will you be able to skip your work here for a morning?" Elizabeth asked. "We can meet in the library after breakfast."

He nodded again. It wasn't really breaking his resolution not to position himself to try to meet her each morning. This was entirely different. He wasn't maneuvering to create a chance to speak to her alone, but rather agreeing to her plan.

She smiled at him, obviously unaware of how she affected him. "Thank you. Until dinner, then, Mr. Darcy." She dropped another curtsy.

"Miss Bennet," he said, bowing. Then she was walking away, the wind sending her hem dancing about her boots and her hair blowing forward into a face he couldn't see with her back turned, but could unerringly picture. Darcy leaned against the stable wall and watched her go.

Chapter Ten

After gathering the eggs, Elizabeth walked quickly back toward the house. She had the oddest sensation that Mr. Darcy was watching her, but didn't turn to look. If he was, the way the wayward wind was blowing her dress against her backside would make meeting his gaze insufferably embarrassing. She yanked at her skirt with her free hand, though it didn't seem to do any good, and hoped he'd returned to his work long since.

Not that he'd really seemed to be working. Yes, he had his coat and cravat off and his shirtsleeves rolled up in that way he'd taken to of late, a state of half dress that did unacceptable things to her ability to think properly. He'd no pitchfork, brush, or any other tools for various horse related tasks about him, though. It was almost as if he'd simply been standing there waiting for her, which was ridiculous. With all that needed to be done to keep Rosings going, Mr. Darcy had too much to do to wait half the morning for a few words with her about chickens.

She entered the bustling kitchen, her mind still on Mr. Darcy as he'd been in the stable yard, dark hair tousled by the wind. He had no right to go standing around the yard in his shirtsleeves, his hair in disarray, where any young miss could see him. Though he was often a bit grim and reserved, surely he couldn't be unaware of how appealing he was, and she did not mean for his station or income. Why, standing in the yard like that, still unwed, was nearly irresponsible.

"Elizabeth," Mrs. Allen said, startling Elizabeth back into the moment. "Thank you, dear. It's kind of you to take this task on yourself. We do need every bit of help we can find to keep this kitchen running as it should."

In fact, Mrs. Allen need not be in the kitchen now that they'd hired a cook, but Elizabeth would never say as much unless the cook protested. It made the widow too happy to be there to rob her of it. "It's no trouble at all," Elizabeth said.

To her chagrin, she had to battle down another blush as she spoke. She felt guilty accepting praise when she knew the only reason she took on the task was to have chance conversations with Mr. Darcy. Worse, she'd somehow felt compelled to lie to him about why she was doing it, in case he suspected, which had only embarrassed her.

Elizabeth handed over the eggs and hurried from the kitchen, displeased with her inner turmoil. She did not, she reminded herself, harbor any ardent feelings for Mr. Darcy. He was highhanded. He was pompous. He'd never apologized for thinking so little of her station and family, or for breaking up Bingley and Jane. None of his crimes had changed.

Though, she respected him now, as she never had before. Not just because of the truths in his letter, but because of his recent actions. Much as she bemoaned the enticing appearance he'd adopted as he saw to farmyard tasks, she was impressed with his willingness to take them on.

Who would have thought that the lofty gentleman who hadn't found her, or any other woman in Hertfordshire, handsome enough to dance with, would be working in a stable of his own free will? Why, where was the condescension now? The aloof arrogance that had so turned her against him from the start? If Miss Bingley could see Mr. Darcy this way she would be horrified, yet every moment Elizabeth spent in his presence warmed her toward him more.

She sighed, then glanced quickly about the hall she walked to make sure no one had observed her. It wouldn't do for anyone to think she was mooning over some gentleman. Especially since she most assuredly was not. His offenses still remained, she reminded herself, listing them again for good measure.

Elizabeth took a moment to collect herself, forcefully setting aside images of Mr. Darcy looking warm and approachable, and made her way to Anne's room. Before her meeting with Mr. Darcy, she wanted to ask Anne's opinion about additional servants. She didn't think Anne would volunteer one, but had been trying to get the mistress of Rosings to take more of an interest in her estate.

Elizabeth knocked on Anne's door. She could hear Kitty within, reading aloud. Waiting for the maid to answer, Elizabeth was unable to help glancing at the entrance to her own room. That conjured up an image of Mr. Darcy as he'd been the night he arrived in Rosings, his eyes dark with appreciation before he came to his senses and left her chamber. Had he still wished to wed her, he could have easily made the incident public and possibly forcing her to marry him. Of course, Mr. Darcy was not a man to do such a thing.

Anne's newly appointed personal maid opened the door Elizabeth stood at, securing her attention. "Yes, miss?"

"Is Miss de Bourgh seeing visitors?"

"I'll ask, miss."

The girl disappeared behind the closed door, but it reopened almost immediately.

"She says she's happy to receive you, miss," the maid said, backing into the room with a curtsy.

"Thank you," Elizabeth said.

Anne's ruffle-bedecked chamber wasn't as stuffy as usual; the curtains thrown wide and the windows cracked open. Elizabeth was pleased to see that, for she privately thought that a lack of sunshine and healthy fresh air was part of Anne's trouble. As often happened, Kitty was sitting in a chair holding a book. What was unusual of late was that Miss de Bourgh was sitting up in bed, propped up by pillows.

"What are you reading?" Elizabeth asked, smiling at them.

"It's called *The Mysterious Hand* and it was written by Augustus Jacob Crandolph," Kitty said. "There's an exciting scene that takes place on a balloon ride. Count Egfryd is really frightening."

"That doesn't sound like a book from Rosings' library," Elizabeth said, amused by Kitty's enthusiasm.

"It wasn't, but it will be now," Anne said. "I ordered it and some others from London after Mother died. I'm glad I did. Kitty enjoys books with a bit of adventure in them, and I find it's more fun to read when I share it with someone."

"I love it," Kitty said. "It's even better than *The Mysteries of Udolpho*. I read that when Miss de Bourgh was sleeping. She's already read it." She gestured to the table beside her.

Elizabeth saw three other books there as well, in addition to a slightly worn looking copy of *Mysteries of Udolpho*. There was *The Life of Samuel Johnson,* a book of poems called *Lyrical Ballads,* and a dictionary of the birds of Kent. "You've been reading about birds?" Elizabeth asked Kitty. That one hadn't come up during dinner yet.

"Miss de Bourgh says that every time I read a novel I should read something that isn't a novel. I don't like that one," she said wrinkling her nose at the bird book. "The others were kind of interesting."

"Papa has books at home," Elizabeth said.

"I never wanted to read them. Lydia wasn't interested in reading," Kitty said.

"As I said, it's more entertaining when you read them with someone," Anne reiterated, smiling at Kitty encouragingly.

Usually, Elizabeth bemoaned that Kitty was a follower, seemingly unable to think for herself and dragged along on every inane idea that popped into Lydia's head. Now, she saw that trait could be turned into an advantage for her younger sister. In following Anne, she'd selected a much better role model. Perhaps, if they could see her wed to a reasonable gentleman, she would follow him into a pleasant life, free of silliness and rudeness.

"I'm sure Miss de Bourgh is entirely correct in both her recommendation and declaration," Elizabeth said. "Perhaps, if we took a walk sometime so that you could see some of the birds you've been reading about, you may even come to appreciate that book."

"Maybe," Kitty said, scrunching up her nose again. "Are you going to stay long? I do so want to find out what happens at the end of this actually interesting book."

"No, not long," Elizabeth said. She shook her head at Kitty's manners. Well, Anne's good influence couldn't be expected to change Kitty entirely. "I came to ask Miss de Bourgh a question about the servants."

"Oh," Anne said, sinking down into her bed. "I'm sure you know the answer better than I do."

"It's a matter of preference," Elizabeth said. "Your preference, so no one can know it as well as you. Mr. Darcy is going to send to London for more servants. I didn't know if you wished to restaff to the extent your mother kept."

"I don't know," Anne said. She seemed almost to shrink. "She did have so very many servants. One couldn't breathe sometimes. I know Rosings has a certain image to maintain."

"Rosings is yours now," Elizabeth said in a gentle tone. "Rosings' image is whatever you wish it to be."

"I simply can't make decisions like this," Anne said. "I don't feel well. Kitty, could you please latch the windows? The air is too chilly."

"Yes, Miss de Bourgh," Kitty said. She set aside the book, glaring at Elizabeth, and jumped up to go close the windows.

Elizabeth sighed. "It isn't a decision that will affect anything," she said softly, so Kitty might not hear. "You can't make an incorrect choice in this. I won't let you have too few servants or too many. I just desire to know your feelings on the matter."

"Really, you will have to decide," Anne said. She draped the back of her hand across her forehead, closing her eyes. "I trust you implicitly, Elizabeth. I need to sleep now, if you'll excuse me."

"Of course," Elizabeth said, trying to keep her annoyance from her tone. She curtsied, though Anne's eyes were still closed, and left the room. Kitty followed her out on soft feet.

"I hope you don't bother Miss de Bourgh too much about the servants," Kitty said, glaring at her. "You've upset her terribly."

"Rosings need a proper staff and Miss de Bourgh should be aware of that, at the least," Elizabeth said. She drew Kitty away from the door, in case Anne's new maid was listening. "Why, her new maid is so green, she likely doesn't even know how to properly arrange Miss de Bourgh's hair for a dinner party, let alone how to help her select garments. As mistress of Rosings, Anne requires a tutored level of service."

Kitty set her lips in a mutinous line. "I have been teaching Miss de Bourgh's maid and assisting Miss de Bourgh. I don't only read to her. I take care of her."

"That's good of you," Elizabeth said, relinquishing the argument. She'd focused on the maid as an example of the situation with the staff, not the only issue. There was no real point in trying to convince Kitty that more servants were needed, though. Obviously, Elizabeth and Mr. Darcy would have to make such decisions.

"It's odd to say, as it seems like it should be a trial to spend all day helping someone and reading to them, but I enjoy it," Kitty said.

"That's good of you too," Elizabeth said.

"You know, Lizzy, I never felt useful at home. I was always the person who was most often ill and people had to help me and I could tell that for you and Jane and Mama and Papa, I was just in the way. Now I know someone who is really ill and I'm helping her, and I'm not in the way at all."

"Oh, Kitty," Elizabeth said, filled with distress at her sister's interpretation of their actions toward her, and guilt at the mildly accurate content of that interpretation. "You were never in the way."

"I was, to everyone but Lydia," Kitty said. "Only, the older we get, the more in the way I am to her, too. She didn't want me to get to go with her to Brighton. She was happy I wasn't invited. No one wants their coughing sister in the way of their enjoyment."

"I can't speak for Lydia," Elizabeth said. "I, for one, am very happy you've come here. You're a tremendous help to Miss de Bourgh and that means you're helping all of Rosings."

Kitty blinked, looking surprised by Elizabeth's vehemence. "It's nice to feel like I'm helping," she said. A grin split her face. "Did I tell you,

Lizzy, Miss de Bourgh let me have another one of her dresses? I have to add a bit to the hem, but she's given me some beautiful lace to do that with. It's too bad you have to remake Lady Catherine's dresses completely because they're so large for you. Miss de Bourgh's are much nearer your size. You'd only have to take them in a bit at the bosom. Maybe if you didn't pester her so much about servants, she would like you well enough to give you one of her gowns."

Elizabeth shook her head. No, she couldn't expect Anne to have changed Kitty completely. Still, it seemed her sister was benefiting more from her association with Miss de Bourgh than Elizabeth ever would have expected. If for no other reason than to thank her for her influence on Kitty, Elizabeth supposed she could stay a bit longer and make a few more decisions about servants.

Chapter Eleven

Darcy strode into the library, leaving the door open to safeguard Elizabeth's reputation, though he couldn't say the thought of closeting them in didn't pass through his mind. She looked up at him and smiled and he reminded himself that her smile meant nothing, weary with the reiteration of that internal mantra. She sat before a table, surprising him with the copious looking notes arranged in front of her. No wonder she proceeded with such efficiency.

"I see you have come prepared," he said, bowing before taking a seat across from her.

"Preparedness, I believe, leads to more fruitful results."

"Undoubtedly," he said. "What conclusions have your preparations led you to?" Aside from that you would be the perfect mistress of Pemberly? He frowned, trying to push that thought from his mind.

"We have several issues to discuss," Elizabeth said, looking down at her notes. "First, there is the disparity between the higher wage we're paying the new servants and the lower one being given those who loyally remained."

"Paying all of the servants the new wage would be costly," Darcy said, though he could see the fairness of it.

"I believe Miss de Bourgh can afford it," Elizabeth said, raising amused eyes from her pages.

Darcy nodded. "She can."

"I also believe it would be only fair to make the raise in pay we'd be giving those who didn't leave effective as of the day Miss de Bourgh took over the estate."

Darcy nodded again.

"Good," Elizabeth said. She set aside several sheets. He could see they contained the names of various servants. "Then there is the issue of those who have returned, seeking their old positions."

"Returned?" Darcy asked.

"A few of those who left have returned, looking quite sheepish, I might add."

"And you believe we should hire them back?"

"I do," Elizabeth said.

Darcy frowned. He wasn't sure. They'd shown disloyalty.

"Everyone was leaving," she said. "For many, handing them a large sum of money is nearly like plying them with drink. It obviously went to their heads and they followed along with the rest. I wouldn't punish them for a momentary lapse in judgement."

"I may."

"Then you and I differ on that," she said, a challenging spark in her eyes. "We need experienced staff who know how to conduct themselves at Rosings. Those who wish to return represent the surest source of such men and women."

She was correct there. He noted that she'd left out that salient point until she'd engaged him in an argument. Had she done it in order to win? As much as he enjoyed debating her, there was little point in drawing out the issue now that he was in agreement with her. Still, the defectors should suffer some penalty. "They shall be under a year's probation in which they can be let go without reason."

"Isn't that the life of every servant?" she asked, amusement leaving her.

"I suppose that depends on the household," he said.

"I take it, then, that is not how you conduct your estate?"

"I would never cast someone out without reason, or without some means of ready currency to help them find their way." His mind flashed to Wickham. He hadn't even sent that reprobate away empty handed. If anyone deserved to be left desolate, George Wickham did.

Perhaps Elizabeth's mind traveled to a similar place, for she abruptly dropped her gaze to her papers once more. "I feel that those who have returned should receive the higher wage as well, but should only receive it from the day they are reinstated, not from the moment Miss de Bourgh became mistress."

"I would see them suffer a bit more for their foolish abandonment of their posts, but I will defer to you on this."

"Thank you," she said. "I believe it will be for the best, so that everyone can integrate peaceably. We don't really want to employ people who harbor resentment."

"True."

"That brings us to the number of additional staff needed," she said. "I don't believe we should return Rosings to the level Lady Catherine kept it until Miss de Bourgh says that's what she wants. Footmen are expensive."

"I believe Miss de Bourgh can afford it," he said, tossing her earlier words back at her.

"Because she can afford it, doesn't mean she will want it."

"Not want it? Why wouldn't she want to live in luxury?" Darcy asked. Was she arguing for the sake of it again, or could she possibly be serious?

"Not everyone considers luxury that important," she said. She flushed, perhaps realizing that her statement could be taken as reference to her refusing his proposal.

"Most people do. Most people would sacrifice many non-material things for living in greater luxury," he said. "You are the only exception I know."

Though he wished to say more, to expound on her virtues, that was the closest he dared come to mentioning his proposal. He took in the conflict on her face. Was she regretting her decision? Had living in Rosings, even in the state it was in, accustomed her to luxury? Was she about to say she'd changed her mind and would be happy to marry for money? If she did, would she still be the Elizabeth he loved? He leaned forward, both longing for and dreading the words.

"You say I am the only person you know of who places luxury

below honor?" she said, her tone low and hard. "I tell you now, sir, I know at least two others."

He looked at her questioningly. Those were not the words he'd expected from her.

"The first is yourself," she said it almost as if the knowledge offended her. "The extent of Miss de Bough's wealth has been impressed upon me. If you value the material more than ethereal concepts such as honor and love, why haven't you wed her?"

"Touché," he said, not bothering to argue that he didn't need any more wealth than he had. It would sound like a boast, and they both knew that wasn't the reason he didn't wed Anne. "And the second?"

Elizabeth's eyes narrowed farther. "My sister Jane. She would not marry simply for wealth."

Ah, the source of her sudden anger. "So you say," he countered.

"Are you doubting my judgment or my honesty?" she asked in a suddenly honeyed tone.

Although she said it sweetly, the steely look never left her eyes. Darcy knew he'd landed himself in a hole now, for he couldn't avoid answering her. "Judgment," he said decisively. He could hardly call her a liar.

"So you believe me to have misjudged my own sister?"

How had he gotten himself into this corner? "I do." He held up a hand when she opened her mouth to speak. "I observed her closely. I did not see signs of true attachment. I believe she would accept an offer from Bingley for the good of you all, setting her own happiness aside. What I did was as good for her as for him."

Elizabeth took several deep breaths. He was very aware that she was struggling not to unleash her temper. He was also very aware that he needed to somehow keep his eyes on hers, not drop them to take in what her deep inhalations were doing to her décolletage. Sadly, he knew she would never appreciate the nearly inhuman effort it cost him.

"Do you know what I believe?" she asked. "I believe you prefer to think my judgment was false rather than admit yours was. You, the great Mr. Darcy, a man much too good to have set foot in Hertfordshire in the first place, could not possibly have been wrong." She glared at him. "I admit I erred in judging you and Mr. Wickham, but you erred in your judgment of me. Neither of us has a perfect record. I knew Mr. Wickham for a few months. I've known Jane my entire life. She loved Mr. Bingley. You owe it to the happiness of both of them to set him straight on that."

"No."

"No?" she bit out.

Darcy frowned. He wished he didn't have to disagree with her on something she obviously felt so strongly about, but in justice to both Bingley and Elizabeth's sister he had to stand his ground. "If I go to Bingley and tell him that I believe your sister truly loved him, there are two possibilities. The first is that Bingley is so easily influenced by me that he will act on what I say, as he did when I advised him against wedding her. If that is the case and I now tell him that your sister loved him, it will be almost as good as telling him to marry her. He will act, not out of love but out of obedience. Would you want that?"

"No," she said. "Yet you cannot convince me that you think Mr. Bingley would marry someone because you told him to."

"Not even if he was almost in love with her, and she had good reason to expect his proposal?" Darcy shook his head. "I've seen him in love many times, and it never lasts." He held her eyes until she looked down.

"You can't have known that would be the case in this instance," she said. He was relieved that her voice was softer, her anger dimmed.

"Let us look at the other alternative," he said, pressing his advantage. "That Bingley never loved your sister, even if she did love him. However much he was attracted to her, he didn't love her very much then and doesn't love her now. Bingley is very obliging, but he is quite capable of acting on his own. How much could he love her if he's never made an attempt to see her after all these months?"

"He loved her last November," Elizabeth said.

"If he still loves her, it is the most tepid love I've ever seen. He could easily return to Netherfield. My comments should not have carried that much weight."

She raised unreadable eyes to his. "Thank you for clarifying your actions."

Darcy scrutinized her, unsure how to respond.

"I believe we're in agreement about everything except how many additional servants to send for from London," Elizabeth said, her tone businesslike. She shuffled through her papers. "As I see it, the fair thing to do would be for you to send for two thirds of the servants required to bring the staff back to what Lady Catherine had. We will then wait to see if Miss de Bourgh requires more. I believe this is the correct way to bridge our difference of opinion. It is not just Rosings and Miss de Bourgh I consider here, for she can hire in more servants at a later date. I'm also taking into account uprooting people's lives to come for a position that may be deemed unnecessary in a short time."

Darcy nodded, feeling bereft. Elizabeth hadn't seemed this withdrawn from him since he'd given her his letter.

"Here is a list of what would be needed to restore what Lady Catherine had." She handed him a sheet from her notes. "I will trust you to adhere to our two thirds agreement."

He took it without looking at it.

Elizabeth stood. "I bid you good day, Mr. Darcy."

Before he could rise to bow to her, she was gone. It was some time before Darcy stood. He folded the paper Elizabeth had given him and tucked it into his coat. He departed the now silent library to go about his day, feeling disheartened.

That evening, for the first time since his arrival, Darcy dreaded dinner. He had no idea what his reception from Elizabeth would be. As he dressed for the meal, he considered again that he was lingering in Kent for too long. Yet, with Anne still ill and the running of Rosings' holdings still in transition, he felt it was necessary for him to stay. All of his Fitzwilliam relatives were hovering over the earl's bedside, even though word had come that he was awake some of the time and eating soup. Darcy could not pass the responsibility of assisting Anne to someone else, because there was no one else.

Nor did he wish to leave things as they stood between him and Elizabeth. Not that he was quite sure how they stood. She hadn't stormed from the library, but he was sure she still didn't agree with him.

Darcy descended, walking slowly to the parlor the ladies favored. As he suspected, it contained Elizabeth and Mrs. Allen but not Miss Kitty Bennet, who'd taken to dining with Anne in her room to keep her company. Both women stood when he entered, dropping curtsies. He bowed, holding out his arm to Mrs. Allen.

"Mr. Darcy, punctual as always," Mrs. Allen said.

Darcy nodded to her without giving a verbal reply. He escorted her down the hall to the dining room, Elizabeth trailing behind.

There were some new footmen now, though Darcy waved the young man on his side of the table back and helped Mrs. Allen with her chair himself. He took his seat opposite Elizabeth, looking across the table at her with mild apprehension. If she was vexed with him, hopefully she had more grace than to show it in so public a place as the dining room.

Elizabeth was not glaring across the table at him as he'd feared. Nor was she even seated, or turned toward him. Darcy followed her gaze.

Anne stood in the doorway, Miss Kitty behind her. The new mistress of Rosings was too thin and too pale. She seemed to hesitate on the verge of stepping into the room, Kitty Bennet hovering at her shoulder. Darcy stood, aiming a bow in their direction.

"Anne, dear," Mrs. Allen said, jumping up and hurrying across the room. She took Anne's hands in her own. "It's so wonderful to see you. Do come dine with us."

Mrs. Allen dragged her cousin across the room and Darcy moved to assist Anne with her chair, once again waving off the nervous looking young footman. By the time he had her properly settled, the other ladies were seated. Darcy followed suit. A maid hurried forward with a place setting for Anne and another for Miss Kitty, who seated herself beside Elizabeth.

"It's good to see you at dinner," Elizabeth said to Anne. "And you, Kitty. We've missed your talk of meadow dwelling birds."

Miss Kitty pulled a face. "You know I don't enjoy reading about birds. I only did so because Miss de Bourgh insisted. Now she's making me read about flowers." She turned worshipful eyes on Anne.

Darcy looked down at the table to hide his amusement.

"Kitty," Anne said in a gentle voice. "Young ladies do not make faces during dinner, and I agree with your sister. We're going to send you on walks so that you may see some of the birds and blooms you've been reading about. It will help you better appreciate the lesson I'm trying to instill, which is that there is much beauty and interest in the Kentish countryside."

"Yes, Miss de Bourgh," Kitty said in dutiful tones. "Will you walk with me?"

"We shall see," Anne said.

Miss Kitty looked hopeful, but Darcy took Anne's words to be a refusal. He stole another look at Elizabeth, but she, who normally would have asked him of his day, avoided his eye. She turned to her sister.

"I will walk with you, Kitty," Elizabeth said. "I would quite enjoy it."

Darcy cleared his throat, wishing he dared offer to accompany them. Servants brought their first course, saving him from what would likely be an embarrassing request. As he ate, he watched Anne. She didn't eat much, but she ate some, which was a good sign.

To his right, Mrs. Allen kept up a steady stream of conversation between bites, mostly with Miss Kitty. The silence at his end of the table, between him and Elizabeth, grated on Darcy. He hoped the others would attribute the lack of conversation to not wanting to exclude Anne. Elizabeth and he both made forays into engaging her in conversation, but were rebuffed.

Anne took a very small helping of the second course, almost as if she simply wanted a taste of everything without actually eating it, but there were enough different dishes so that she ate almost a third of a meal. Darcy had more than enough time to observe his cousin's actions, as Elizabeth didn't speak to him and avoided his gaze for the remainder of the meal. He ate stoically, wondering if dinner would ever end. Laying down her fork, Anne turned to him.

"I understand Mr. Whitaker has been helping. Perhaps you should invite him for dinner," she said.

"Of course," Darcy agreed. He narrowed his eyes at her choice of topic. Did she wish the man to court her? He would be an excellent choice for managing Rosings' farmland. He wasn't wealthy, but he seemed a decent, hardworking, helpful gentleman.

Anne turned to Mrs. Allen. "Is the kitchen up to it?"

"Yes, but the meal will be simple."

"I thought we were near to full staff in the kitchen," Anne said. "The food was good tonight."

"Oh, we are," Mrs. Allen said. "The cook we have is local, however, and not up to your late mother's fashionable standards. Miss Elizabeth said, and I agree, that there is no need to send to London for a fancy cook and kitchen staff if you are happy with what we have."

"I prefer it. The food my mother's cook made was overly rich for everyday. Will our new cook be prepared for the occasional more elaborate meal or rich dish?"

Mrs. Allen looked to Elizabeth.

"Not yet," Elizabeth said. "She's very capable, but not accustomed to such a grand kitchen or elaborate access to ingredients and staff. She plans to practice some of the old cook's recipes, however, and hopes to have enough ready soon."

"I'm sure Mr. Whitaker will not mind a simple fare," Darcy said. Not if the man was being given the opportunity to court Anne. He'd be a fool to let a simple meal ruin such a chance.

"See to it, then," Anne said, rising from the table.

They all stood. "You're retiring?" Elizabeth asked, looking worried.

115

"I am tired," Anne said. Ignoring the bows and curtsies directed at her, she slipped from the room.

"I best go read to her," Miss Kitty said. "She likes to be read to before she sleeps. Excuse me."

To Darcy's surprise, Miss Kitty dropped a curtsy before hurrying away. It was pleasant to see the girl's manners improving. What wasn't pleasant was the silence that descended. Darcy wished his manner weren't quite so refined, for he very much wanted to cut his dinner short too.

The awkwardness between him and Elizabeth was straining, but fortunately didn't last long. By the following day, she seemed herself once more. He wasn't deluded into thinking that meant she'd come round to his line of reasoning or that she'd forgiven him. It was obvious she was perfectly willing to contain her displeasure for the sake of comradery. It pained him to think it, for he'd thought she was growing more fond of him, but such ease in ignoring a vehement disagreement with him must mean she didn't care very much.

Three days later, Mr. Whitaker came to dinner, after an enthusiastic acceptance of Darcy's offer. Anne joined them before the meal began, seeming stronger but still frail. Although she'd requested the man, as far as Darcy could tell, she hadn't taken any special care with hair or dress, but that could be due to the inexperience of her maid.

As they entered the dining room, Anne took her place at the head of the table, seating Darcy to her right, as usual, and Mr. Whitaker to her left. Darcy was a bit surprised she hadn't reverted to a more formal seating arrangement with a guest present, but he wasn't about to complain. To his pleasure, even though it was a happiness underscored by pain, the addition to their seating arrangement placed Elizabeth beside him. Miss Kitty was seated across from her, on Mr. Whitaker's left. Knowing his cousin had invited Mr. Whitaker so that she might come to know him better, Darcy felt he'd be free to devote most of his time to speaking with Elizabeth.

116

"I hear you've been of great assistance to Rosings, Mr. Whitaker," Anne said. "I would give you my thanks."

Whitaker ducked his head, looking respectably humble in the face of praise. "I was merely conducting myself as any considerate neighbor would."

"Still, not all were as conscientious as you," Anne said.

Darcy thought that was an understatement. Most hadn't helped much at all and no one had done as much as Mr. Whitaker. He'd learned the man bore a familial sense of obligation to Rosings, but his efforts went above even the requirements of that.

"As an outdoorsman, you must greatly esteem the Kent countryside," Anne said.

"I do," Whitaker replied. "I know I have my bias, but no other part of our great country can rival the beauty of Kent."

"I am not much for the out-of-doors myself," Anne said. "Miss Kitty, however, has been studying the bounty of our fair county."

"Have you, Miss Kitty?" Mr. Whitaker asked, taking his cue to turn to her.

She looked up from her plate, obviously startled at being addressed. Darcy narrowed his gaze as Mr. Whitaker's smile widened. He glanced at Elizabeth, who was watching the exchange closely.

"I've been reading an awfully great deal about Kent's birds and flowers," Miss Kitty said.

"And do you enjoy reading of them?" Whitaker asked.

"Not really," Miss Kitty said. Her eyes widened the moment the words left her mouth. She set down her spoon. "That is, I prefer to read tales of adventure. Descriptions of plants and birds are a bit . . ." She floundered, shooting a look across the table at Elizabeth. "I suppose it is nice to read what the flowers mean, in case anyone ever brings me any."

"Yes, it is," Anne said, intervening. "Not to mention, as we've discussed, once you see the things you've been reading of, you'll appreciate better what you've learned."

"But no one ever has time to walk with me," Miss Kitty said. Her voice was a bit breathless, her eyes still on Mr. Whitaker, who hadn't turned to Anne.

"I promise to walk with you tomorrow, Kitty," Elizabeth said.

Whitaker turned a charming smile on Elizabeth. Darcy frowned at the man. Was he there to flirt with every young woman at the table?

"I would be honored to join you both on your walk, if I may?" Whitaker said, his tone full of entreaty.

Taking in the man's charming smile, Darcy resolved that he would be on that walk as well, and any other walk which included Mr. Whitaker. He was not allowing Elizabeth to throw away her intelligence and beauty on a small landholder in a back corner of Kent. He'd thought he liked the man, but he wasn't as sure now. Why did Whitaker have to be so damn affable, and look at Elizabeth like a hound begging for its favorite treat?

"And we would be honored to have you, sir," Elizabeth said, adding to Darcy's ire.

The meal continued in a like vein, Darcy saying little as Whitaker engaged both Miss Bennets. Later, as they all lingered over the remains of the dinner, he felt a gentle touch on his arm. Looking down, he realized Anne was trying to gain his attention and felt a stab of guilt. Seated beside her, he should have been attempting to entertain his cousin, not hanging on every word of Elizabeth's conversation with Miss Kitty and Whitaker.

"Don't glower like that," Anne said in a low voice. "You'll scare him off."

Darcy eyed her. So, she hadn't wanted Whitaker there for herself. She was playing matchmaker. Well, she could go play it with someone other than Elizabeth.

"Do not interfere in this, Darcy," Anne said. Her voice was still low, but held more steel than he'd ever heard her employ before. "This is my way of thanking her for her kindness."

Darcy sat back in his chair. He knew he was still frowning, but he couldn't help himself. Why shouldn't Elizabeth come away from her time in Rosings with a match? She must marry. All young women must. Who was he to stand in her way? Whitaker was a worthier gentleman than most.

"Shall we retire to the parlor, ladies?" Anne said, standing.

Her words prompted a polite departure of the ladies, leaving Darcy alone with Whitaker. They headed to a nearby drawing room to take their port. Ignoring strict propriety, Darcy strolled to the window with his, looking out onto the grounds, using the lingering summer daylight to assess the level of care they were being given. He knew he needed to gather his composure before he could exchange pleasantries with the other man.

Unfortunately, Whitaker obviously didn't realize that. He strolled over to join Darcy at the window. "The grounds look to be in hand again," he said. He took a sip of his port. "Excellent port."

Darcy nodded, though he hadn't yet sampled it. He was sure all of the port his aunt had kept was deserving of the praise.

"About Miss Bennet," Whitaker said, his tone tentative. "What sort of family is she from?"

"Her father is a small landholder in Hertfordshire," Darcy said, struggling to keep his tone even. "There is a mother whose family is in trade and three more sisters. The estate is entailed, so they will have little when Mr. Bennet expires."

"I see, so not much in the way of a dowry," Whitaker said. "A wife who's not of the gentry and five daughters to marry off with little to recommend them other than their looks, which I must say seem exceptional from all I've seen. Poor fellow."

Darcy took a sip of his port to keep from speaking the words that sprang to his lips. Elizabeth was worth much more than her small dowry, whatever the sum. He drew in a breath. Of course, Whitaker wasn't a man of great fortune. He would need to carefully consider what his bride would bring to his household.

"I wonder if she has anyone waiting for her, back in Hertfordshire,"

Whitaker said in a quiet voice, as if speaking to himself.

"Not that was apparent when I visited there this past year."

"No? A sweet faced miss like that, with such an endearing lack of conceit, and no suitors? Hertfordshire must be overfull of women with few gentlemen to spare."

Darcy nodded, working not to grind his teeth.

"It was endearing, wasn't it, the way she was so surprised that I turned to speak with her? As if she's accustomed to being ignored. Of course, with an older sister like Miss Elizabeth, one could see how that would be."

Whitaker's words slowly registered.

"Do you suppose they hold to all that nonsense of the elder sisters wedding before the younger? How many of the five are older than Miss Kitty? A man might have to wait some time for four girls to find husbands."

"Miss Kitty is the second youngest, but I don't think Mr. Bennet would be particular on that matter. Even if he chose to be, his wife would not allow it." Darcy felt a lightness in his heart. Elizabeth would still be free. The man was a fool for preferring Miss Kitty, but Darcy thanked providence for it.

"Of course, I daresay at least one of the older sisters might be married soon," Whitaker said, giving Darcy a meaningful look out of the corner of his eye.

Ah, so the man wasn't a fool, but perhaps a keen observer. He thought that Darcy had intensions toward Elizabeth. If only that could be true. "We should rejoin the ladies."

"That we should," Whitaker said with a friendly smile.

Chapter Twelve

The following day, Mr. Darcy joined Elizabeth and Kitty on their walk with Mr. Whitaker. Elizabeth wanted to still be angry with Mr. Darcy. He was so wrongheaded in some of his views that it was nothing short of infuriating. Yet, if they didn't address but a few delicate topics, he'd come to be her favorite of companions.

So, as she was resolved not to address said topics on their walk, they spent a very pleasant time following Mr. Whitaker and Kitty about. Mr. Whitaker pointed out various flowers and birds, and Kitty seemed genuinely enthusiastic. Anne would have been more successful, Elizabeth thought, if she'd combined educational books for Kitty with educational walks. The books alone were not enough.

Their walk seemed to set a precedent because after that they walked whenever the weather permitted. Elizabeth quite enjoyed herself, but the frequency and increasing length of their walks drove home that neither she nor Mr. Darcy must truly be needed in Rosings any longer. Not if they had time to spend so frivolously.

Though the walks revealed to her that she might be able to consider her obligation to Anne ended, and she missed her father and Jane, Elizabeth knew she couldn't leave quite yet. Not when Mr. Whitaker was clearly courting Kitty, who'd never before had a suitor. Though Kitty wouldn't be alone should Elizabeth leave, she didn't feel Anne or Mrs. Allen would provide enough in the way of chaperoning. Anne could hardly be stirred from her books, nor Mrs. Allen from the kitchen.

So Elizabeth remained, and knew why she remained. What she didn't know was why Mr. Darcy did. He undoubtedly had his own affairs waiting. He'd already done more than any cousin could be expected to

121

do and had likely saved Rosings from ruin.

Did she dare hope that he remained simply because of her? She'd come to value his company quite highly. She looked forward to those moments each day when she could see him. In her heart of hearts, she realized she'd come to care, and lamented the fact.

What good could come of caring for Mr. Darcy now? She's missed the opportunity to be his. There was no conceivable way he would propose a second time. A man who has once been refused! How could I ever be foolish enough to expect a renewal of his love? Is there one among the sex, who would not protest against such a weakness as a second proposal to the same woman? There is no indignity so abhorrent to their feelings!

The more walks the four of them took, the more Elizabeth regretted her refusal of Mr. Darcy's offer. She was coming very close, she realized, to being quite in love with him, something she could not allow. Unable to deny herself the enjoyment of spending time with him, she instead endeavored to harden her heart, keeping her greatest grievance with him always present in the back of her mind; his adamant refusal to tell Bingley what he must be allowed to know about Jane.

She might be failing Jane by not convincing Darcy to speak to Mr. Bingley, but Elizabeth was resolved not to fail Kitty. Therefore, as Mr. Whitaker's attention to Kitty didn't seem to be diminishing, she decided she must know more about the man. The next time they walked, she deliberately slowed her pace, falling well behind Mr. Whitaker and Kitty, though still keeping them in sight.

Elizabeth looked up to find Mr. Darcy training a questioning glance her way, obviously noting her abnormal pace and wondering what was behind it. She wet her lips nervously. For all the easy comradery they'd achieved, speaking on matters of the heart with Mr. Darcy still seemed a bit awkward.

"Please tell me about Mr. Whitaker," she said. There was no point in mincing words. "Why has he been so concerned with Rosings? Was it his original intension to court Miss de Bourgh, do you think?"

He blinked, as if rearranging his thoughts. Did she imagine the disappointment that flickered in his eyes? What had he supposed she'd lingered so far behind the others to speak to him of?

"His father was a good friend of Sir Lewis de Bough," Mr. Darcy said, his tone even. "Mr. Whitaker the senior died about three years ago." He gestured toward where Mr. Whitaker and Kitty meandered, nearly out of sight. "This Mr. Whitaker didn't get along with Lady Catherine."

Elizabeth resisted snorting at that or commenting that it was understandable.

"There was no real rift, but he didn't visit. Mr. Whitaker has a nice little property, perhaps fifteen hundred pounds a year," he added. "He is the only son. His three older sisters are all married and he is the youngest child."

"What do you know about his character?"

"Nothing bad. He gave Rosings more real help than any of the other neighbors. Lady Catherine was not popular."

"And since people were denied access to the local heiress, there was no reason to come."

"True," Mr. Darcy replied.

Elizabeth looked up the path, where Kitty and Mr. Whitaker had stopped walking and spoke together quietly. "I hope you don't think I'm gossiping. I mean only to investigate. As her only relative near, I am responsible for Kitty."

He nodded. "I'm glad your sister has become such good friends with Anne. Lady Catherine didn't really allow her to have friends."

"That's sad. I've had Jane and Charlotte." Jane's name reminded Elizabeth of Darcy's role in her favorite sister's current unhappiness.

By the tightening of his mouth, she guessed that Darcy recognized that. "Mr. Whitaker told me that his father felt his friendship with Sir Lewis made him responsible for Lady Catherine and Anne," he said, gratefully not addressing the more volatile topic she'd inadvertently raised.

"Do you mean that Mr. Whitaker's father was responsible or that Mr. Whitaker is responsible?"

"The father first, and after his death the son. He told me that our responsibilities are not always limited to the people we like. He said that Miss de Bourgh didn't need his help as long as her mother was alive, but he felt an obligation to help her now."

"He sounds like a good person."

"I've never heard anyone speak ill of him."

"And you are such a gossip that everyone tells you every scandalous story," she teased, eliciting a slight smile. She looked away, searching for Kitty and Mr. Whitaker. It was dangerous to be alone with Mr. Darcy when he smiled like that.

"I've just been gossiping with you," he replied in an amused tone.

"Tisk. We've already established that I am a concerned relative investigating my sister's suitor. I daresay you have so little experience with gossip you can't separate the two."

"You cannot convince me you have so much."

"I have four sisters," Elizabeth said. "It would be impossible for me to avoid it, no matter that I do try."

"I have but one sister. She's in as much need of a friend as Anne was before Miss Kitty arrived."

"Yes, and you said Miss Darcy is enamored of the pianoforte?" Elizabeth said, quickly steering the conversation to a safe topic, for the look he directed at her was oddly intent.

"She is. Georgiana plays well, I am pleased to say."

Mr. Darcy allowed the shift in conversation and they continued their walk in harmony. Later, when they returned to Rosings and bid the gentlemen farewell, Kitty followed Elizabeth to her room. Elizabeth didn't say anything as they walked the halls. Kitty likely wished to speak of Mr. Whitaker, and that wasn't a conversation for corridors. Once they were closeted in her room, Elizabeth turned to her sister, only to find Kitty glaring at her.

"I saw you back there making eyes at Mr. Darcy, Lizzy," Kitty said.

"How can you enjoy spending time with that man? You know how he treated Mr. Wickham."

Elizabeth pursed her lips. She hadn't thought to disclose Mr. Wickham's lies to Kitty, wanting to shelter her younger sister from the truth. Yet, if Kitty was old enough to be courted, she should no longer be treated as a child. "Mr. Wickham was paid three thousand pounds when he asked to give up the living he'd inherited. He has no complaint against Mr. Darcy."

"I suppose you learned that from Mr. Darcy." Kitty's tone was skeptical, her brows raised.

"Let's suppose I didn't learn anything from Mr. Darcy," Elizabeth said, surprised at Kitty's reaction. It had become so clear to her that Darcy was by far the better man, she wondered that everyone didn't see it. "The very first evening I was in Mr. Wickham's company, he asked me what I thought of Mr. Darcy. I told Mr. Wickham I disliked him."

"As do I," Kitty said. "He called you plain and wouldn't dance with anyone."

"Yes, but consider this: Once I declared my dislike to Mr. Wickham, he told me all about what Mr. Darcy supposedly did to him. Meanwhile, he said that he could never publically expose Mr. Darcy out of respect for Mr. Darcy's father. This was after knowing me for less than a day. How was he to know I wouldn't tell everyone? If he told Mama this, or if I did, the whole county would know it in a week."

"Yes..." Kitty said, sounding uncertain.

"Mr. Wickham also told me he would not back down from Mr. Darcy, but he didn't attend the ball at Netherfield. Does that not speak of a man steeped in guilt?"

"Mr. Wickham wanted to avoid a scene," Kitty protested.

"I think you know that Mr. Darcy would not have created one," Elizabeth said, holding Kitty's gaze.

Her sister frowned. "I suppose not. He hardly speaks at all, except to you. He doesn't seem as if he'd want a whole ballroom full of strangers attending to him."

"And let us not forget," Elizabeth said, pressing her advantage. "Mr. Wickham told everyone about his supposed mistreatment after Mr. Darcy left, when it was likely that Mr. Darcy would never be in the neighborhood again, not giving him a chance to know of the slander, let alone refute it."

"I guess," Kitty said, looking confused.

"When they first saw each other that day we were walking to Meryton with Mr. Collins, Mr. Darcy turned white and Mr. Wickham turned red. Which one do you think was embarrassed and which one was angry?"

Kitty didn't respond, her eyes wide and worried looking.

"Wickham started courting Mary King when she inherited ten thousand pounds. He ignored her before that," Elizabeth said, adding her last, most telling piece of shareable evidence.

"Lydia's seeing a lot of him," Kitty blurted out.

That wasn't good, Elizabeth thought. "Could you write her and tell her about Wickham?"

"She wouldn't believe me."

"Try," Elizabeth prompted, but she knew Kitty was right. Even assuming Lydia wasn't too headstrong to listen to anyone, she led and Kitty followed. "Thank you for telling me." She smiled at her sister, trying to ease the worry that now lined her face. "Maybe I'll write Papa. You should go see Miss de Bourgh and then ready for supper."

Watching Kitty leave, Elizabeth tried to reassure herself that Wickham would do Lydia little harm since she had no money. She racked her mind for something she could do. She could write their father, but that would likely prove useless, since he would do nothing. Their mother would do less good, possibly even encouraging Lydia. Elizabeth sighed, hoping nothing would come of Kitty's revelation, but filled with dread nonetheless.

Chapter Thirteen

The following day, as Elizabeth and Kitty joined Mr. Darcy and Mr. Whitaker in the foyer in preparation for their walk, Colonel Fitzwilliam arrived. Elizabeth thought he looked quite well, showing no ill effects from having been worried for his father. Of course, they'd had letters saying the earl was recovering well, so there was no longer any reason to worry.

"Why, good of you all to come out to greet me," the colonel said, stopping in the doorway to look around at them. "Though, in truth, I can't say I'm familiar with all of you."

"Richard," Mr. Darcy said, bowing to his cousin. "May I remind you of Mr. Whitaker. I believe you've met him once or twice. He lives nearby and has been of great assistance to Rosings in this time of need. Mr. Whitaker, Colonel Fitzwilliam, my cousin."

"It's good to know someone's been picking up my slack," the colonel said with a bow for Mr. Whitaker.

"I am sure I've only done what any neighbor would," Mr. Whitaker said. "Mr. Darcy has done all of the real work."

"May I also present Miss Bennet's younger sister, Miss Kitty Bennet," Mr. Darcy continued.

Kitty dropped a curtsy. Elizabeth was pleased with how naturally done the gesture was, and with the demure turn of her gaze. Nothing like the Kitty that Lydia encouraged.

"Miss Kitty Bennet, it is an honor to meet another of the exceptional Bennet sisters," Colonel Fitzwilliam said, bowing.

"Thank you, Colonel," Kitty said. "It's a pleasure to make your acquaintance. My sister has spoken highly of you."

"You must all be headed off somewhere," Colonel Fitzwilliam said.

127

"Don't let me keep you."

"We were about to take some fresh air," Elizabeth said. She glanced at Mr. Darcy, wondering if he would invite his cousin to accompany them. It would be rude not to, but Darcy was the most appropriate person to invite his cousin to join them. Secretly, she hoped the Colonel would say no, for she was sure he'd end up walking with her and Darcy.

"Would you care to join us?" Mr. Darcy said after casting a look at her.

"No, thank you," Colonel Fitzwilliam said. "I shall get cleaned up and present myself to Anne. She's well?"

"She is," Mr. Darcy said. "May I assume from your arrival that your father is now fully recovered?"

"He is, but he'd have only himself to blame if he weren't. He tripped over one of my mother's pugs, you see. That's what went awry. When Mother received the letter about Lady Catherine's death, she shrieked as if the devil himself had walked into the parlor. My father came running and tripped over her favorite pug, breaking his arm and hitting his head. It didn't look good for a time, let me tell you, but he's recovered nicely. Tough old thing, my father."

"Your mother must have been mortified," Elizabeth said. She couldn't imagine how wretched she'd feel if she'd done something as silly as shriek over bad news and gotten her husband injured in the process. "I'm so pleased to hear your father is well."

"They tell me mother was quite upset." A twinkle lit his eyes. "They also say she actually seemed more worried about my father than that dratted pug. Who would have thought? She loves her dogs more than her children, and I should know."

"Was the pug hurt?" Kitty asked.

Elizabeth hid a smile. Apparently, Kitty would side with the Colonel's mother when it came to the value of a prized pug.

"Only startled. My father says that if no other good comes of the incident, at least the pug's been improved. It used to be the dog made

128

my father walk around it. Now it gets out of his way."

"Smart dog," Darcy said.

"He would have been smarter if he'd learned to get out of people's way earlier," Elizabeth said.

"True enough," Colonel Fitzwilliam said. "I won't keep you from your walk any longer, but I'll leave you with this thought, Darcy: Let me know what responsibilities I can takeover. Now that my father is recovering, there's no reason you should have to bear the burden of Rosings alone."

"Thank you, but you exaggerate," Mr. Darcy said. "Elizabeth has been managing most everything here, with the help of Anne's cousin Mrs. Allen in the kitchen. Mr. Whitaker has been assisting me with the estates." He glanced at Elizabeth. "In truth, I don't think either you or I will be needed here much longer. Things are nearly back to the point of running themselves with just the occasional look in from us."

Elizabeth made sure her expression remained neutral. She was surprised how much she disliked the idea of them all departing Rosings. She should be excited to return to Jane and her father, but she would miss Mr. Darcy terribly.

"Glad to hear it, glad indeed," Colonel Fitzwilliam said. "I knew the two of you would have things well in hand. Feel bad for running off on you, though."

"You did what you had to," Mr. Darcy said firmly.

"Kind of you to say. Now enjoy your walk. Don't let me keep the lot of you standing in the foyer all day."

There was a flutter of bows and curtsies, and soon Elizabeth found herself walking beside Mr. Darcy, Kitty and Mr. Whitaker some little ways in front of them. She smiled up at the blue sky, enjoying the slight breeze. It was grand to be out of doors. Rosings was running well, as Mr. Darcy had said. The weather was perfection, with summer in full bloom. She walked beside a tall, distinguished, handsome gentleman. There was little that could make the day any more pleasant.

"What do you smile at?" Mr. Darcy asked in a low voice.

Elizabeth glanced at him askance. "Why, Mr. Darcy, are you asking after my thoughts? I'm not sure that's entirely appropriate."

"Appropriate can go to the devil," he said. "I want to know what brings you the joy I see upon your face. Is it that my cousin is returned?"

Was he jealous? "What if I said that walking on a fine spring day, in fine company, is the source of my smile?" she said. Her heart thudded in her chest and she realized how important his response was to her.

"I would say that while I would never dream of declaring you a liar, I find it difficult to credit such a notion."

Elizabeth stopped. He took one stride without her and then turned back around to face her. She moved closer so she could keep her voice low. "I assure you, sir, that it would be nothing but the truth. A fine day, in such pleasurable company, is what brings this feeling of joy I have."

"Then, may I derive that you no longer abhor spending time with me?"

"How can you think it?" she said, alarmed he should. "Have we not spoken most every morning in the yard, dined together every night, walked together every day of late?"

"I'd hardly allowed myself to hope this was because you have come to prefer my company," he said.

He looked down at her with his intense, unfathomable gaze. Elizabeth's breath caught. Hope? Did he mean he still hoped she would come to care for him? He hadn't relinquished all feeling for her, then? He leaned toward her.

"May I, Elizabeth?"

"May you what, Mr. Darcy?" she asked breathlessly. His use of her first name suggested an intimacy she wasn't sure she wanted.

"Dare to hope?"

"I don't know," she said, distressed at her own answer. She didn't know. When he'd proposed to her months ago, she had three objections to him: his behavior to Wickham, his personality, and his separating Jane and Mr. Bingley. She was wrong about Wickham and she now liked him, possibly even loved him, but could she love a man who'd destroyed the happiness of her sister? Should she love him?

"Elizabeth, Mr. Darcy," Kitty called. "Do keep up. Whatever are you doing back there, dawdling like that?"

From the amusement in Kitty's voice, Elizabeth knew her sister could quite well imagine what they were doing, speaking too privately, and she very well wished Kitty would leave them to it. Mr. Darcy searched her face for a moment. He started to turn away. Elizabeth put a staying hand on his coat sleeve and he swung back, brows raised in question.

"I really don't know. There is still the issue of Jane and Mr. Bingley," she said. As she said it, she saw the hope leave him. He would not give in on this issue.

"Elizabeth," Kitty called, closer this time.

Elizabeth made to remove her hand from Mr. Darcy's arm, but he clasped his over it. "At least your opinion of me has improved," he said, carefully adjusting her fingers to lay properly along his arm. His hand on hers was a surprisingly intimate gesture. They turned up the path to face Kitty and Mr. Whitaker. Kitty came to a halt, casting a grin at her walking companion. "And I can enjoy your company without the fear that you are only tolerating me for the sake of harmony at Rosings," Darcy said too quietly for Kitty and Mr. Whittaker to hear.

"That you can." Elizabeth raised her chin, refusing to blush. If only they could resolve the one thing that came between them. She loved Jane too well to give in on the point, even for Mr. Darcy.

"Come on then," Kitty said. Mr. Whitaker offered her his arm. She took it and they turned back up the path. "Do try to keep up this time Elizabeth, Mr. Darcy," Kitty said over her shoulder, her tone a mixture of officiousness and mischief.

Elizabeth looked to Mr. Darcy, embarrassed by her sister's behavior and how justified it was. He smiled warmly down at her. Shifting her attention to where her hand rested on his arm and then back to the bright spring sky, Elizabeth returned his smiled and they resumed their walk.

Later, when they returned to Rosings after Mr. Whitaker tended his farewells for the day, they found Colonel Fitzwilliam, Anne and Mrs. Allen seated in the parlor. Anne looked up from the book she held as they made their greetings. Colonel Fitzwilliam lowered his newspaper, but not for long. Mrs. Allen exchanged pleasantries without dropping a stitch.

"The post arrived. There are letters for all three of you," Anne said, her expression warm. "I hope you had a pleasant walk."

Elizabeth had the oddest urge to blush, though Anne couldn't mean anything by her statement.

"I think Elizabeth had a very pleasant walk," Kitty said, giggling.

"Young ladies do not giggle in mixed company, Kitty," Anne said in a tone of mild reprimand. "Was it a particularly pleasant day, then?"

"The weather is very fine," Elizabeth said, shooting a glance at Kitty. "You should walk with us, Miss de Bourgh. We needn't go farther than you like. The weather is beautiful. It's not too hot for summer."

"Perhaps tomorrow or the day after," Anne said. "Your letters are there." She gestured to a silver tray that had been left on a side table.

Elizabeth crossed to the table, finding a letter from Jane, which she took, and one from Lydia, which she handed to Kitty. "There is one from your sister as well, Mr. Darcy," she said. "Would you care to read it now?"

"I would," he said.

Elizabeth brought him his letter, trying not to find the action intimate. He didn't seem to. His visage and tone were the same as always, aloof and unreadable. He seated himself on the remaining sofa, far to one side, as if daring her to sit with him. As the only other option remaining was beside Mrs. Allen, Elizabeth took his dare. It wouldn't do for Kitty to sit with Mr. Darcy, after all. Kitty cast her a knowing smirk and took her place beside the window.

Elizabeth opened her letter from Jane, stealing a glance at Mr. Darcy. Could his words that afternoon mean anything other than that he still had an interest in her? Would he be writing a letter soon, to her

132

father? She glanced down at Jane's careful writing, guilt tugging at her. She wanted Mr. Darcy to propose again, and she longed to say yes, but what of the wrong he'd done Jane? What of his disdain for her standing and her family?

"Oh, no," Kitty whispered.

"What's the matter?" Elizabeth asked.

Where she sat beside Mrs. Allen, Kitty had gone white. "Lydia is planning to elope with Mr. Wickham," she said, sounding almost as if she might cry. "She says they're going as soon as he can sell her necklace and get money for a carriage. They're going to Gretna Green."

"He'll never marry her," Colonel Fitzwilliam said. He folded his paper, a frown pulling down the corners of his mouth.

"But why take her to Gretna Green then?" Kitty asked.

Darcy and Colonel Fitzwilliam exchanged glances but didn't speak. Elizabeth was trying to find a delicate way of saying what no one else was willing to say. She wished Colonel Fitzwilliam had been a little more careful with his words.

"Wickham has a history of being fond of having a woman share his bed," Anne said.

Kitty gasped. Elizabeth turned to Anne. She didn't know if she was more shocked that Anne knew such a thing or that she would say it aloud. She could see by their surprised expressions that Mr. Darcy and Colonel Fitzwilliam were equally stunned by their cousin's words.

"My mother didn't always know when I was listening," Anne said, shrugging. "The question isn't why he's taking her, but what can be done."

"They may have already left," Elizabeth said. What could be done? The full ramifications of Lydia's actions hit her. Why, they would all be ruined. No one would marry her, Jane, Mary or Kitty if Lydia ran off with Mr. Wickham and shared his bed. She went cold, a feeling of dizziness stealing over her. Worse, if he got her with child.

"I don't think they would have left yet," Kitty said. Her voice sounded far away to Elizabeth. "Lydia wrote that Wickham had some kind of duty that would keep him busy for a while, and it will take time to sell her necklace." She sighed. "I always liked that necklace. I told Mother she should have given it to me. I'm older, after all."

Elizabeth surged to her feet. Something must be done. This couldn't be allowed to happen. Crossing to Kitty, she held out her hand. "Let me see?"

Kitty turned over the letter, her eyes going wide. Elizabeth imagined her face was giving too much of her distress away to her younger sister, but what good would shielding Kitty do? Once Lydia ran off with Wickham, there would be no shielding any of them from the repercussions.

Elizabeth stood there, trying to read the letter, but the words blurred together. She was aware of both Colonel Fitzwilliam and Mr. Darcy coming to read over her shoulders.

"Would an express to Colonel Forster work?" Elizabeth asked, unable to think of anything else to do.

"Anne, can you arrange that?" Mr. Darcy asked. "I'm going to go there myself. I may beat the express."

"Yes, I can," Anne said. "We can also send an express to Mr. Bennet."

"I'll write it," Elizabeth said. She hurried over to the writing table in the corner. "May I use your stationary, Anne?" Her writing things were in her room. Logically, she knew the time it would take to get them wouldn't change a thing, but she desperately wanted to have the letters written and on their way.

"Of course," Anne said. "Will you write both letters, please? I'll send for someone to take them immediately." She rang for a servant.

Elizabeth started writing, her hand a bit shaky. She was aware of Mr. Darcy and Colonel Fitzwilliam leaving the room, but didn't look. A servant came and went, and another. She didn't hear what Anne said to them, focused on the two brief letters she must write and address. When she finished them, she turned to find a footman waiting silently behind her.

As he was walking out with the letters, Mr. Darcy entered, dressed for travel. "Miss Kitty, may I take the letter?"

"You may. Elizabeth has it," Kitty said.

Elizabeth looked down, seeing Lydia's letter on the desk. She hadn't even realized she'd carried it over with her. Mr. Darcy strolled toward her and she stood, proffering it.

"What manner of monster is he?" she whispered. "How can he do this thing?"

"He is the worst manner of monster," Mr. Darcy said. He squeezed the hand she held out before sliding the letter from her cold fingers. "But he will not do this thing. I won't allow it."

Elizabeth nodded. She tried to smile, but knew it didn't work. She wanted to believe him. If anyone could fix the situation Lydia had created, she was sure Mr. Darcy could.

"Elizabeth," he said in a low voice. "No matter what happens, you have my assurance that you will be well." With a fierce look in his eyes, he swung away, long strides carrying him from the room.

Chapter Fourteen

Richard told Darcy that he would sleep while Darcy's coachman Alderson drove so that he could take over after several hours. Darcy envied Richard's ability to sleep under such circumstances. He was too filled with anger at Wickham to rest. Darcy supposed his cousin had learned the art of sleeping under any sort of pressure while serving in Spain.

They changed horses as often as they could, making good time. Richard took over for Alderson after sleeping for a few hours, saying that a tired driver could be dangerous. After several hours, Darcy felt compelled to take over for Richard, though he hadn't slept.

In his youth, Darcy had briefly wanted to become a member of the Four Horse Club, but his father had protested based on the inanity of their rules. He'd said it was one thing to aspire to drive four horses well, but another thing to follow a set of meaningless rules about how to dress just to show off that you were accepted by a certain group.

As he drove, Darcy wondered if his father would approve of his quest to save a silly girl from Wickham. He decided his father would. Darcy's family had allowed Wickham to become what he was. Although Darcy did not have personal responsibility, he had a familial one.

Nevertheless, when Darcy drove into Brighton at dusk he was only thinking about how Wickham's actions could affect Elizabeth, not about family responsibility. After a brief inquiry, they found Colonel Forster at home. He was going over some paperwork with his aid, a Lieutenant Pratt, who Darcy recognized from his stay with Bingley the previous fall.

"Colonel Fitzwilliam and Mr. Darcy to see you, sir," the aid who showed them in said. "I wouldn't have disturbed your work, but they say it's a matter of some urgency." The young man saluted and backed from the room.

"Colonel, Mr. Darcy," Colonel Forster greeted. He and Lieutenant Pratt both stood, bowing, though confusion showed on Forster's face.

"We're sorry to barge in on you, Forster," Richard said. "We're here on a delicate, yet rather urgent, matter."

"May I ask the nature of the matter?" Forster asked.

"It pertains to a young woman in your household, a Miss Lydia Bennet," Richard said.

"Miss Lydia Bennet?" Forster asked, frowning. "I can't see what business you might have with her."

"Darcy, the letter," Richard said.

"You probably saw Miss Lydia spend time with her sister, Miss Kitty Bennet, when you were in Hertfordshire," Darcy said, pulling the letter from his pocket.

Colonel Forster nodded.

"Miss Kitty is staying with a cousin of mine," Darcy continued. "Miss Lydia wrote this letter to her sister. I have folded it to show the relevant paragraphs."

He handed over the letter. Forster's frown deepened to a scowl as he read. He unfolded the letter, turning it over and then back, obviously assuring himself of the authenticity. Handing it to Pratt, who started reading, he stood and crossed the room. Forster leaned out the door, yelling for his wife. Darcy winced. Forster sat back down, tapping his fingers on his desk.

Pratt handed Darcy the now folded letter. "Excuse me," he murmured.

Forster nodded and the lieutenant left. Moments later, a surprisingly youthful woman stuck her head into the room.

"You called for me, dear?" she said in contrite tones and Darcy realized she was Mrs. Forster.

"Bring Miss Bennet down here at once," he told her.

"She went to bed early with a megrim," Mrs. Forster said.

Darcy hoped that was true, but found that Mrs. Forster's words ended all optimism he'd harbored of arriving before Wickham put his plot into motion.

"Get her now," Colonel Forster barked.

Mrs. Forster scurried away.

Darcy glanced after the retreating woman. Colonel Forster's manners were a bit lacking, yet even with his abrupt nature and being a man used to giving orders, he didn't seem to be succeeding in taming Miss Lydia Bennet. What hope had a man like Mr. Bennet ever truly had, especially with his wife encouraging Miss Lydia at every turn? "A letter was sent to Mr. Bennet right after we left Kent," he said.

"Good, but she is my responsibility while she is here." Forster frowned at them. "I knew they'd danced several times, but I had no idea Wickham would try something like this."

"The man's a bounder," Richard said.

Mrs. Forster came running into the room, holding a letter that she thrust into her husband's hands. "She's not in her room and she left me this. She's running away with Wickham," she gasped out.

"When did you last see her?" Forster asked, his eyes scanning the letter.

He handed it to Darcy, who took in the brief lines, holding it so Richard could read it as well.

"Less than an hour ago, I think," Mrs. Forster said. She wrung her hands. "I should have known something was amiss. Lydia never has a megrim."

No, she just causes them, Darcy thought. He folded the letter and dropped it on the desk. He tucked Miss Kitty's back inside his coat. He would return it, though the thing ought to be burned.

"Your carriage is ready?" Forster asked, looking between Darcy and Richard.

Darcy shook his head. "The horses aren't fresh."

"Where did Pratt go?" Colonel Forster looked around. "Pratt! Where the devil is he?"

"Coming, sir," a voice called from down the hall. Mrs. Forster stepped aside as Pratt came running in. "I may have done the wrong thing," he said breathlessly, "but I ordered four horses saddled. They should be here in a few minutes."

"Perfect. Good man," Forster said. "Now go ask around. Find out if anyone had seen that devil Wickham or Miss Bennet. Catch up to us as soon as you have something. We'll be headed north."

"Yes, sir," Pratt said. "I'll start with the staff." He saluted smartly and hurried from the room.

Forster led the way outside. True to the Lieutenant's word, four horses were being walked up. Darcy, Richard and Forster took three, heading north out of town. They weren't on the road long when Pratt caught up with them with a description of the carriage and confirmation they were headed in the right direction.

As they rode, Darcy realized it was likely they would catch Wickham and Miss Lydia before long. Wickham probably wanted to preserve the horses but get reasonably far that night. That would mean going slowly, in spite of the light of the nearly full moon.

They slowed their mounts to a walk to rest them. It was more important to keep them fresh and avoid injury than to catch Wickham a bit sooner. Now that they were behind him on the road, and he in a coach with no idea they were in pursuit, the outcome was almost certain.

Colonel Forster reined his horse in to drop back and come alongside Darcy. "I don't quite understand. Why would Wickham elope with the girl rather than ask Mr. Bennet for her hand? From what I recall, he's five daughters to marry off. I'm sure he wouldn't turn down a redcoat for one of the lot."

Darcy forced down his anger at Wickham, keeping his voice controlled. "Wickham has always been eager to have young women share his bed, but a dowry like Miss Bennet's isn't likely to tempt him to marriage. He probably has debts here and in Meryton, and knows himself well enough to realize he'll rack up many more. Wickham has always fancied himself a wealthy wife to end his financial troubles."

140

Colonel Forster looked shocked. "I hope you are mistaken. I've known the man to be a bit lazy, but not a cad." He looked Darcy up and down. "What is your role in this?"

"I know Wickham and his character well, yet I didn't warn others. Had I, this may have been prevented. Also, he was my father's protégé and I feel responsible for any harm he does."

Darcy hoped Colonel Forster wouldn't ask him if he had other reasons, although there was truth in what he'd said. He did have an obligation to his father's protégé, even if he didn't like or respect him. He was simply leaving out that about which he didn't wish to speak. He didn't want to divulge his interest in creating very close ties to the Bennet family. Though he would wed Elizabeth no matter what scandal her sister embroiled herself in, he still hoped to save the woman he loved the pain such familial disgrace would bring.

They increased their pace again, putting an end to talking. While he rode, Darcy thought about what he wanted to do to Wickham. His mind went through fists, swords, and pistols. Each possibility gave him considerable satisfaction. Wickham had never worked hard at anything. Darcy was no longer interested in boxing, but he'd taken it seriously for a couple of years, as he still did fencing and shooting. He was considerably better than Wickham at all three.

By the time they slowed their horses again, Darcy had worked his way through every imaginable retribution and his anger had begun to lose its fierce edge. Much as the thought of hurting or even killing Wickham pleased him, he realized the fact that he could beat Wickham meant he wouldn't try. To challenge him would be murder, and a more gentlemanly death than Wickham deserved.

Darcy ground his teeth. Why did being a gentleman mean he had to be so sensible? Why couldn't he let his anger go and attack Wickham, scum that he was?

He knew the answer, of course. Years of reading the best masters hadn't been squandered. Darcy was civilized, even if Wickham wasn't. Yes, Wickham lied, racked up debts and had tried to elope with

Georgiana. Yes, he was obviously willing to seduce a gently bred, very foolish, young lady. None of that excused Darcy from his responsibility to behave properly. He would not take advantage of his superior strength and skill. That was not the mark of a gentleman. Wickham's worth did not dictate how Darcy should behave. His own did. He wasn't willing to compromise his honor for the likes of Wickham.

Really, there was only one way in which Wickham was superior. He was able to get along with people. Was Darcy jealous of him? A little. He was jealous of Wickham's easy charm. Darcy remembered Elizabeth telling him before he proposed . . . what was it? That he should practice his social skills more. He took solace in knowing, though, that while Wickham made friends easily, his basic dishonesty meant he didn't keep them. Darcy had never alienated a friend through improper behavior.

"That looks like it," said Pratt, interrupting Darcy's rambling thoughts.

Pratt urged his horse to greater speed. Darcy saw what he was planning and came up on the other side of the carriage. Each one of them grabbed the reins of a horse and, as if they'd rehearsed it, they pulled the carriage to a halt. The driver made no attempt to resist, his eyes wide as he took in the four men surrounding the coach, with two being in uniform.

Richard and Forster came up to the carriage doors, one on each side, and yanked them open.

"Miss Bennet, when you were invited to stay with me, I expected you to behave properly," Forster barked into the carriage.

"But we're going to be married."

Darcy recognized the voice as Lydia Bennet.

"Not without your father's permission, you aren't," Colonel Forster said.

"George said we could get his permission afterward. Besides, he has some silly debts or some such, so we had to leave," Miss Lydia said.

Darcy grimaced at her inanely cheerful tone.

"My father will give permission," she continued. "I've been alone with my Georgie in a closed carriage for more than an hour."

"Colonel Fitzwilliam, how good to see you."

The oily charm in Wickham's voice grated on Darcy.

"Can't say the same," Richard growled. "Sit over there, Wickham. I'm riding with you."

Richard dismounted and Darcy moved up to take the reins of his horse. He caught a glimpse of Wickham's back as he started to switch seats, then Richard filled the doorway, climbing in. Darcy urged his horse around to the back of the coach, where he could tie the extra mount.

"I don't care how long you've been in a carriage with him," Forster was saying to Lydia. "You are coming back to Brighton with us now. Move over, Miss Bennet. I'll be chaperoning you on the return drive. Mr. Pratt, if you could take my horse?"

Pratt did so and Colonel Forster got in the carriage.

"How did you find us?" Darcy could hear Miss Lydia ask as he secured Richard's horse. "I would have sworn Harriet wouldn't enter my room until morning. I told her I had a terrible megrim and would sleep in."

"You wrote your sister," Richard said. "She showed the letter to Darcy who decided you needed rescuing."

"And he sent you?" Wickham's tone dripped derision. "Darcy uses his father's money to hire people to do things because he cannot do them himself."

Darcy realized Wickham must not have seen him. Neither Colonel corrected Wickham's misapprehension. He didn't mind. Maybe, for once, he would gain honest knowledge of what Wickham said about him instead of a courteously tempered rendition.

"Did Mr. Darcy tell you I can't be allowed to marry George?" Miss Lydia cried. "He has no right to order us about. He hates my Georgie because his father loved George better."

"He always misrepresents me to his own advantage," Wickham added.

Darcy nearly had to admire the man. Wickham's words would be the exact truth, if Darcy had spoken them about Wickham. The man lied so easily, it bordered on a pathology.

"Mr. Darcy's feelings toward Wickham have nothing to do with you being permitted to run off with a man while under my roof," Forster barked. "I've had about enough of this. Pratt," he called in an even louder voice. "See that this carriage gets us back to Brighton."

From where he lingered behind the coach, Darcy could see Forster reach out and close the door. Richard closed the other. As they rode slowly back, Darcy amused himself by envisioning the scene inside the carriage. Wickham was across from his commanding officer, whose guest he'd run off with and next to Richard, of whom he'd always been a little afraid. It was a fitting first step in punishing the man.

Darcy hung back when they arrived in Brighton. Neither of the runaways appeared to notice him when they disembarked the carriage. Colonel Forster ordered some soldiers to help Pratt lock up Wickham. He then walked a tearful Miss Lydia into the house.

She looked back, likely searching for Wickham, and her eyes alighted on Darcy. He could tell by the surprise and anger that transformed her features that she recognized him. He wasn't sure if she realized he was one of the men who'd stopped the carriage. Colonel Forster marched her upstairs to lock her in her room. Mrs. Forster looked on with grim satisfaction. When Colonel Forster returned, Mrs. Foster handed him a note.

After reading it, Colonel Forster turned to Darcy and Richard. "Your coachman has arranged lodgings for you both at the Lion Inn. I'll order a meal for us. After we eat, Pratt can take you there and bring your mounts back. You are welcome to stay here, if you prefer."

"The inn is fine," Darcy said, glancing at Richard.

Richard nodded in agreement.

"You should know that on the ride back, with some prodding from Colonel Fitzwilliam, Wickham admitted that the story he told about you was a lie."

"What story?" Darcy had never learned what Elizabeth had believed he'd done to Wickham.

"He put it out that you arbitrarily denied him a valuable living that your father wanted him to have. In the coach, Wickham admitted that you paid him three thousand pounds for it and that he came to you with the request."

"Was that why Miss Bennet was crying?" Darcy had assumed it was because she'd been caught. "Wickham's falsehood was revealed?"

"I don't think the fool girl would care. No, she was crying because when I put it to him, Wickham refused to marry her. He said he'd never offered her marriage and had never planned to marry her. He'd only asked her to run away with him."

That was a cruel thing to admit in front of the lady, even by Wickham's standards. "I thought that once cornered he would wed her," Darcy admitted. A cad like Wickham could do worse than the attractive and chipper, if addle brained, Miss Lydia. Not to mention, usually Wickham would do anything to save face. "Mr. Bennet isn't rich, but he could probably cover Wickham's debts."

"Wickham still thinks he can marry an heiress," Richard said dryly. "This did not please Miss Bennet."

Darcy shook his head. Wickham was a fool. "Will you be writing her father?" he asked Forster.

"I'll do it now. I would rather get it over with. Let me order our meal first."

Although Darcy wanted a bed more than a meal, he politely waited for Colonel Forster to write the letter and then sat down to the meal provided. To Darcy's surprise, Colonel Forster had Lieutenant Pratt join them. Mrs. Forster did not, saying she'd already dined.

"What will you do with Wickham?" Richard asked as they settled into their meal.

"For now, I'll keep him locked up," Forster said. He speared several vegetables with his fork. "To safeguard the lady's reputation, I told people he's been jailed because I learned he has many debts in Meryton and that he's been accumulating more in Brighton." He glanced at Darcy. "As I'd only your statements on that aspect of his character to go on, I thought at first I might have to eat my words, but one of my corporals told me that he was surprised I hadn't known about Wickham's Meryton debts."

Darcy said nothing. There was no need to emphasize that he was honest and Wickham was not. He was tired of explaining that to people.

Richard grunted. "I assured you as much. He's always been a reprobate. It would be a surprise if he changed."

"I assume Miss Bennet's father will be coming here," Colonel Forster said, looking at Darcy.

"I would think so," Darcy said. Mr. Bennet was an indolent father, but Darcy hoped the letter Elizabeth had sent would have Mr. Bennet already on his way.

"Let's assume he does come. What do you think he'll want done? I might be able to force Wickham to marry Miss Bennet, but I'm not sure that's a good outcome for anyone. Wickham may end up in debtor's prison someday. Miss Bennet is a silly fool, but she was under my care. I don't want to face her father and tell him that his daughter has to marry such a man."

Darcy frowned. In spite of Wickham's words in the coach, marriage between the two was now the only course, wasn't it? In this one thing, he would see Wickham behave with honor.

"May I suggest an alternative?" Lieutenant Pratt said.

"You may," Colonel Forster said.

"I have no idea of what to do about Wickham, but I have a suggestion for Miss Bennet. Under certain conditions, I would marry her."

"You would marry her?" Richard echoed.

Pratt nodded, his expression one of resolve.

"What conditions?" Forster asked, the surprise on his face mirroring Darcy's own.

"From you, a promotion to captain, sir."

"I'd lose the best aide I ever had," Forster complained.

"Put that on the write up for his promotion," Richard said, grinning.

"What else?" Forster asked.

Darcy couldn't read the expression Forster had schooled his features into, but he hoped the man was considering it. He hadn't known Lieutenant Pratt for long, but it was already obvious he'd make a much better husband than Wickham. Darcy would like to see this thing done for Elizabeth, so she wouldn't have to worry about her sister. To his surprise, Pratt turned to him.

"Mr. Darcy, you said you feel some responsibility for Miss Bennet because you didn't publicize Wickham's character," Pratt said. "Would you be willing to arrange for a special license?"

"Yes, but why not banns?" Darcy asked.

"Miss Bennet might agree to marry me in the next couple of days because she's angry with Wickham, but I've observed her to be relatively fickle in her affections. In a few weeks, she might change her mind. I want that captaincy."

Darcy nodded. He agreed with Pratt's assessment of Lydia Bennet. Judging by the respect on their faces, the two colonels did as well.

"Do you have a notion of what I can expect in a dowry, sir?" Pratt asked, still looking at Darcy.

"Fifty pounds a year from her family while both parents live. After that, her share of the five thousand pounds settled on her mother." Darcy hoped the rumors circulated in Meryton were accurate when it came to the monetary situation of the Bennet family. Of course, in view of their lack of accuracy with regards to him, it was a lot to hope.

"Why are you willing to marry her?" Richard asked, frowning. "There must be easier ways to get a captaincy."

"Not for me. I've been saving, but it will take years to save enough and by then the war might be over. I'm a second son and have four sisters who were dowered. My parents have no more money for me." He turned to look at the small fire that was burning low in the hearth. "Miss Bennet is a silly thing, but she's always cheerful and undeniably pretty. I want a wife, but can't afford one on lieutenant's pay."

"She doesn't know how to save." Darcy felt compelled to warn the man.

"She's young enough to learn," Pratt said.

Darcy nodded. He hoped so, for Pratt's sake. "I'm willing to do my share of this," he said, pointedly looking at Colonel Forster.

"I think the two of us can arrange a captaincy for Mr. Pratt," Richard said.

Colonel Forster sighed. "You were bound to leave me eventually," he said. He held out his hand to Pratt and they shook. "Assuming Mr. Bennet agrees, I now need to decide what to do about Wickham. I don't want to initiate an action to send one of my officers to debtors' prison."

"If you want to have a weapon to make Mr. Wickham agree to something, I have an idea," Darcy said. Even though Wickham hadn't agreed to wed Miss Lydia to save face, Darcy still knew the man's greatest weakness. Wickham was obsessed with the appearance of respectability.

"What do you suggest?" Forster asked.

"Public humiliation," Darcy said.

Across from him, Richard grinned.

Chapter Fifteen

Darcy's idea took a little work. The first step was to find an artist who could draw an accurate depiction of Wickham. The artist worked while Wickham was sleeping, because they'd all agreed the plan would work better if they could spring it on him. The final portrait wasn't particularly flattering, but it was reasonably accurate.

It was harder to find someone to convert the portrait into a woodcut, but Darcy eventually found the appropriate craftsman. He decided the first run would only be fifty copies. Printed above Wickham's picture were the words, "Mr. Wickham does not pay his debts." Below the picture were the words, "Make him pay in cash. Warning: he may change his name or hairstyle. He has blue eyes, medium brown hair, and a faint two inch scar on the outside of his right wrist."

The day after the first print run, Darcy received a note from Colonel Forster saying that Mr. Bennet had arrived in town. Darcy wasn't surprised when, the following day, Mr. Bennet called upon him at the Lion Inn. Darcy had rented two rooms adjoined by a sitting room for himself and Richard. Since his parlor allowed more privacy than the taproom, he received Mr. Bennet there.

"I wanted to thank you for rescuing my daughter," Mr. Bennet said once greetings were exchanged and refreshments declined.

"I felt I owed it to her. My reserve kept Mr. Wickham's true character from being known," Darcy said.

"I doubt whether your reserve, or anybody's reserve, can be answerable for the event," Mr. Bennet replied. His clipped words revealed his anger. He ran a hand over his face, clearly trying to calm himself. "I'm sorry that my family has participated so willingly in the spread of the lies Wickham told about you."

Darcy shrugged. He'd long since learned to ignore people gossiping about him. With his wealth, it was a fairly common occurrence and to be expected when he entered a small community such as the one in Hertfordshire.

"I don't know if anyone else will tell you, so I feel I must, indebted to you as I am," Mr. Bennet said. "Wickham's been defaming you from his cell. He claims you are incapable of doing anything yourself and use your father's money to cover your incompetence."

"I heard a version of that," Darcy said with another shrug, knowing Wickham felt he should have a large chunk of Darcy's father's money.

"Well, if Forster's or Pratt's description of events are true, you certainly weren't incompetent."

"Everyone contributed," Darcy said. He was not being modest. His wealth had allowed frequent changes of horses, but others had contributed to the rescue as well.

Mr. Bennet looked uncomfortable. He coughed into his hand. "He's also trying to malign your sister, claiming she agreed to elope with him."

Darcy surged to his feet. "He's what?" he demanded. It was one thing to spread rumors about him and to try to bring down his character. He could defend himself. It was quite another matter to harm Georgiana in any way. Maybe he would reconsider dueling the man.

"Don't worry," Mr. Bennet said. "No one believes it, especially since you were seen driving into Brighton and riding out of it. His obvious lies on one subject call into question the validity of his other claim. He doesn't even say that he was ever out of the sight of a chaperone with your sister. He's saying it was in whispered conversations while the chaperone was across the room and on walks when she walked behind them. No one here is taking him seriously."

"That's good to know. I would not like that story to get out," Darcy said, retaking his seat. "Forgive my reaction." With its truth, that story was more dangerous than Wickham's lies.

"Think nothing of it," Mr. Bennet said. "I don't believe you have much to worry about, truly. After I received Elizabeth's express, I sent a note to Mr. Phillips asking him to check with a few local merchants. He sent me a reply before I left the next morning. Wickham owes money. Phillips checked discretely, but the fact that questions were asked will probably make the merchants go public. I don't think Wickham's credibility will be high in Meryton, since his credit is so poor."

"I still don't like the idea of rumors floating around." Darcy felt compelled to give this man more truth than he likely should. "Miss Darcy took a holiday in Ramsgate and Mr. Wickham spent some time with her. I came unexpectedly and Mr. Wickham left the area with a certain alacrity."

Mr. Bennet regarded him in silence. Darcy hoped he wouldn't ask for any more information.

"In that case it is obvious what happened," Mr. Bennet finally said. "Mr. Wickham hinted at elopement and Miss Darcy or her chaperone decided you should intervene." Mr. Bennet cocked his head to one side. "Miss Darcy?" He paused. "Her chaperone?" Apparently reading something in Darcy's expression, he continued, "Miss Darcy wrote you and told you she knew Mr. Wickham was a close friend of the family but she wasn't happy in his company. After receiving her letter, you came posthaste. Relieved that you were there to keep her from the unwanted attentions of an old family friend, she was absolutely delighted that you removed her promptly from his presence." A twinkle lit his intelligent eyes. "I have this from an unimpeachable source that isn't you. I assume I can say the chaperone was removed for not handling the situation herself."

"I would prefer you not say anything to anyone," Darcy said stiffly. He wouldn't condone a lie, even to mislead people about what he wanted concealed.

"Oh, I only plan to tell one person," Mr. Bennet said.

"Your wife?" Darcy guessed, narrowing his eyes.

A slow smile came to Mr. Bennet's face. He shrugged.

"I don't approve of that," Darcy said.

"Fortunately, I don't need your approval. You should know," Mr. Bennet hurried on, not allowing Darcy to speak, "that Lydia is now Mrs. Pratt. They were wed this morning. I understand I have you to thank for the expediency."

Darcy dipped his head in acknowledgement. "Pratt made the request of me. I saw no reason not to assist. Congratulations on your daughter's marriage."

"Thank you," Mr. Bennet said. He regarded Darcy for a long moment. "You seem quite willing to assist my family. I imagine you have your reasons, of course."

Darcy nodded again, hoping Mr. Bennet wouldn't press for them. How could he tell the man he would do anything to spare Elizabeth pain, including make sure her foolish youngest sister didn't bring disgrace to the family? Darcy had no intension of sharing his innermost thoughts, especially when Mr. Bennet would surely construe too much. Nothing was sure between him and Elizabeth, and perhaps nothing would ever come of his regard for her.

"I shouldn't keep you any longer," Mr. Bennet said, standing.

Darcy stood as well. They shook.

"Thank you again, sir," Mr. Bennet said and quit the room.

Darcy retook his seat, mulling over their conversation. He couldn't believe he'd agreed to Mr. Bennet's lie. Or had he agreed? What he hadn't done was insist that Mr. Bennet not spread the story. He could have been more forceful, though he had no hold over Mr. Bennet other than one of gratitude, and Mr. Bennet thought he was doing Darcy a favor.

Once Mrs. Bennet got the story, a version of it would be all over Meryton in days. Darcy found himself hoping that the version was the one Mr. Bennet had given him. There was a certain irony in the lie as it was like Wickham's lies: surrounded by truths. Darcy didn't approve of Mr. Bennet's tactic, though, and knew rumors could take on a life of their own and become something even more harmful. As he hadn't done enough to stop Mr. Bennet, he supposed there would be justice in that happening, but it was Georgiana who would truly suffer.

Georgiana did not deserve to suffer. The only thing his sister had done wrong was agree to an elopement. She had not eloped. She was never alone with Mr. Wickham, by her word and Mrs. Younge's. Although both had reason to lie, he believed his sister. Suddenly, the truth didn't seem so bad. The truth was that whatever his sister had briefly agreed to, she'd changed her mind. If the scandal got out, the harm would not be great. People would forgive her, especially if he secured a strong willed, intelligent, likable sister for Georgiana to help smooth the way to acceptance.

The odd thing was, Mr. Bennet's falsehood was very nearly the truth. His sister could have agreed to the elopement to stall Mr. Wickham while waiting for her Darcy's rescue. It wasn't the wisest move, but no outsider could deny that was the case. Of course, he knew she'd never written him, but no one else did.

Darcy shook his head, casting aside the temptation of letting Mr. Bennet's story stand unrefuted. He would not lie. He would not stoop to Wickham's level. If the story came up the next time he was in Meryton, he would correct it. His conscience was such that he may even journey there expressly for the purpose.

In truth, Wickham didn't know the harm he'd done his reputation by putting the story out. In the past, one of the main reasons Darcy hadn't warned people about Wickham's true nature was concern that Wickham would retaliate just as he was. Wickham knew that Darcy would go to lengths to protect Georgiana from having to endure the repercussions of what had happened in Ramsgate. Now that Wickham had spoken about it, it was no longer a weapon. Darcy was free to speak the truth.

He would have to warn Georgiana, of course. She would be embarrassed, but not truly harmed. He worried it would exacerbate her shyness, but there was little to be done in the regard. His mind returned to the notion of the help a new sister could be to Georgiana in enduring what was to come. In spite of his worry for her, he found himself smiling

153

as he once again pictured the perfect woman to bring into their lives. His life.

Darcy looked up at the sound of the parlor door opening. Richard stuck his head in. "Darcy, there you are. I told Forster I'd fetch you. He's about to interview Wickham and he asked if we would come."

"Of course," Darcy said, standing. He didn't relish the thought of seeing Wickham, but he imagined there would be some satisfaction in telling the man how they'd arranged to stop what amounted to thievery from the merchants of England.

They returned to the colonel's, neither his wife nor the new Mrs. Pratt in evidence. Darcy assumed the latter was now safely with her husband. They were shown into Forster's office by a lieutenant Darcy didn't recognize.

"Mr. Darcy, Colonel Fitzwilliam, thank you for coming," Forster said, standing to greet them. He gestured toward two chairs, which now stood on one side of his desk, facing an empty stool in the center of the room. "If you'll kindly be seated, we can begin."

"Let's get to it," Richard said, sitting.

Darcy joined him, nodding to Forster in greeting.

Two soldiers brought Wickham in and pushed him down onto the stool. He was unshaven, but still maintained his customary air of nonchalance. He saluted both colonels. He glanced at Darcy and nodded, a lazy smirk on his face.

"Wickham," Forster said. "You're here so that I can decide what to do with you."

"Do with me, sir?" Wickham said. He leaned forward, his face eager. "I've done nothing wrong."

"Actually, while you've done nothing illegal, I can't say it wasn't wrong," Colonel Forster said. "No officer in my regiment can be permitted to run off with a girl, especially not one under my personal protection."

"I realize I must put that right. I've reconsidered my earlier words, spoken in haste," Wickham said. "I would be happy to marry Miss

154

Bennet. She may be angry with me now, but if I'm given a chance to talk to her, I'm sure she'll change her mind."

"That option is no longer on the table," Richard said. "The former Miss Bennet married Captain Pratt this morning."

Wickham almost fell off his stool.

Darcy kept his face impassive, but he was grimly pleased to see Wickham's shock.

"Captain..." Wickham trailed off, looking about in a slightly frantic manner.

"Pratt," Colonel Forster supplied.

"Pratt is a captain now? How were they able to wed so quickly?" Wickham bit out, scowling. He shot Darcy an angry look.

Darcy was sure he could follow the other man's thoughts. If Wickham had known he could get a captaincy out of it, he would have begged to marry Lydia Bennet from the moment they were caught. He could tell from the anger in Wickham's gaze that he also suspected Darcy of obtaining a special license, and likely of paying for the captaincy, though Darcy hadn't had to do that.

"There is a ship leaving for Spain in two days," Colonel Forster said, recapturing Wickham's attention. "You will be on it, with the rank of ensign."

"I don't think so," Wickham said, his smile back. "I think I'll resign my commission and leave Brighton."

Darcy stood up and handed Wickham three of the prints with his picture on them. "I had fifty made for the first run. I intend that every shopkeeper has one in any town you visit."

Wickham looked at the fliers and blanched. "I'll never be able to buy anything again. You can't do this to me." He hesitated, and then said with a smile. "It's libel."

"It's only libel if I've lied." Darcy said. "I hold all of your bills from Lambton. I bought your tailor's bill in Brighton, to make sure I have evidence. That should be enough to defend me against such a charge. It isn't as if you can't buy anything. You can go into any shop in England

and pay cash. No one will stop you."

"Cash?" Wickham cried. "I have no cash." He surged to his feet to glare at Darcy, his fist clenched at his sides.

Darcy eyed Wickham, whose attempt to stare him down was made much less effective by the nearly five inches Darcy had on him. Darcy allowed himself a slight smile. He could tell Wickham wanted to hit him. He half hoped the man would try.

Wickham took a step back. "If you put those out, everyone will realize I'm not coming back to pay them. I've left debts from here to York." He looked to Richard and Forster beseechingly. "They'll throw me in debtor's prison."

"They can't reach you to put you in debtor's prison if you're on that ship," Richard said.

Wickham cast a beseeching look about the room again. He took another step backward, sitting down hard on the stool when his legs came up against it. With a groan, he covered his face with his hands.

Two days later, Darcy stood on the docks with Richard, Mr. Bennet and Colonel Forster. They watched in silence as the ship they'd put Ensign Wickham on sailed out to sea, headed for Spain. Once it reached a spot that was too far away for someone to jump off and swim to shore, they turned to face one another.

"Gentlemen, I cannot thank you enough for what you've done," Mr. Bennet said. "I knew Lydia wouldn't be happy until she embroiled herself in some sort of scandal. I'd no idea she would select one which might have had such far-reaching repercussions for her sisters. Having known Lydia her entire life, I still underestimated the extent of her foolishness, and selfishness."

Darcy looked to Richard and Forster, uncomfortable with both the thanks and Mr. Bennet's frankness.

"Always happy to help, of course," Richard said. "I'm afraid I must be off now. I've business in London." He bowed to Mr. Bennet and shook Forster's hand. "Till next time, Darcy," he said, turning to stride away.

Darcy watched him go, thinking it would be a much quieter ride back to Kent. He'd offered to accompany Richard to London, providing his cousin the comfort of a carriage, but Richard had declined. The one thing they'd agreed on was that there was no reason for both of them to return to Kent. Rosings was well in hand. Darcy's return was merely a formality. At least, that's what he'd told Richard.

"Are you returning to Hertfordshire tomorrow?" Colonel Forster asked Mr. Bennet.

"By way of Kent," Mr. Bennet said, to Darcy's surprise. "My daughter wants my permission to marry someone she met there and I haven't yet been introduced to the man."

Darcy stared at Mr. Bennet. How could the man have made no mention of that? Surely, he didn't mean . . .

"At least this one asked," Forster said with a good-natured grin.

Mr. Bennet winced slightly. "Yes, she did. She appears to be more responsible than her sister."

"Mr. Whitaker?" Darcy asked abruptly, hoping the other two men didn't hear the strain in his tone. It would not do to ask which daughter, but Elizabeth was the responsible one.

Mr. Bennet nodded. "That is the gentleman's name. Do you know him? Will he be suitable for Kitty? I can't imagine he will be, as he must be silly to ask for her hand."

"I know him," Darcy said. His relief was so strong, he could almost ignore how Mr. Bennet always disparaged his younger daughters. "He's a worthy gentleman. Not that it is my place to observe such things, but I think you'll find Miss Kitty somewhat changed for the better by her time in Rosings."

Forster shot Darcy a look that clearly conveyed his agreement that Darcy had no right to speak to Mr. Bennet in such a way or on such a topic. Darcy ignored the colonel.

"I can only hope you are correct," Mr. Bennet said. His tone was amused, not reprimanding.

"I am returning to Kent," Darcy said. "Would you care to share my carriage?"

"Thank you," Mr. Bennet said, nodding.

They bid Colonel Forster farewell and selected an hour at which to depart. Darcy left the dock well pleased with how their solution for Wickham had worked out, and even more pleased that he would see Elizabeth again soon.

Chapter Sixteen

Elizabeth perched on the edge of a couch, watching Kitty read a letter from Lydia. It was all she could do not to snatch the note from her sister's hands. A glance told her Anne wore an amused smile on her face, though Miss de Bourgh kept her eyes on her book.

"I would have thought you'd be a faster reader by now, Kitty," Anne said. "It's a good thing Elizabeth is so very patient.

"It's hard to read Lydia's handwriting," Kitty said, looking up from the letter. "It's always abysmal."

"Be charitable," Anne said. "When you arrived here, your handwriting was not so fine as it is now." Anne's insistence that Kitty practice her handwriting was the most recent way she'd decided to improve her guest.

"What does Lydia say?" Elizabeth blurted. Didn't Kitty understand how important it was that Lydia had been stopped from ruining them?

Kitty handed her the letter, looking a bit startled. "You needn't yell at me. All is well."

Elizabeth shook her head. She would make that assessment herself. She dropped her eyes to the page.

My Dear Kitty,

So much has happened since I last wrote! Do you know, I did run off with Mr. Wickham, just as I told you I would, and I am married, just as I said I'd be, but not to Wickham. Isn't that a lark? I bet you never could have guessed I'd do it, especially after you warned me.

I must say, in regard to that, that for once you were completely in the right. I should have listened to you, but I was wholly taken in by Wickham. I thought he loved me, but he didn't. Why, he wasn't ever going to marry me. Can you imagine? How dare he run off with me with no intention of being honorable about it!

Fortunately, I was rescued by my darling Pratt, two colonels, and that awful Mr. Darcy. It was very exciting, but at the time I was so upset about Wickham that I didn't really appreciate what was happening. Now that I'm married, I don't suppose I'll get the opportunity for any more daring rescues in my life. Isn't that a sad thought?

Elizabeth closed her eyes in silent supplication. Sad thought indeed. If Lydia dared do anything so foolish again, she didn't deserve a daring rescue.

You'll never believe it but Pratt, you know, the quiet one who hardly ever danced with either of us, he came to me and told me that he's always loved me and that he was sorry that Wickham was so disrespectful of me. He said he wanted to protect me so I would never need to be rescued again.

Isn't that romantic? Who knew? I mean, of course I always suspected he liked me, all officers do, but I had no idea of how much he cared. He said he wanted to marry me, but thought it was too soon for me to marry him, since I would need time to recover from Mr. Wickham's betrayal. My dear sweet Pratt said that if I agreed to marry him, he would wait until I was sure I was doing the right thing.

Then Harriet Forster came in, interrupting us. She sent Pratt away, but I quickly said yes, so he would return. She is no fun at all anymore, Kitty. You're lucky you aren't here with her. She lectured me endlessly about how I was ruined and how

160

ungrateful I was. She said I would be sent home in disgrace and, if she had her way, I would be treated like a child and not allowed to go to dances or anything until all of my sisters were married. When I told her that no one would want to marry Mary, she said, "Good. Maybe by the time you are thirty your father will let you attend dances."

I was so upset, I started to cry. I didn't want to do it, but I couldn't help it. You should have seen the smug smile on her face. It was horrible. I was glad when she left.

Later, Papa came and said he gave Pratt permission to marry me if I agreed. He said he was a little reluctant, because I was too young to marry. He thought I should stop attending parties and spend my days helping around the house and learning accomplishments. I told him I was not too young. I said I would marry Pratt immediately if I had a chance. Papa said, "Don't be silly. It will take weeks."

Of course, that only made me angry with him. I am not silly, nor am I a child. I proved that to all of them when I married my Pratt.

You see, the next morning Pratt came to me and told me he had a special license! I asked him how he got it and he said that a man who is eager can accomplish a lot. He said he wanted to marry me right away in case Papa changed his mind.

We got married that very morning! We showed Papa he was wrong. I'm the youngest and now I'm married first. If I go back to Longbourn, when we go to dinner, Jane must go lower, because I am a married woman. And now I can sign with my new name!

Your loving sister,

Lydia Pratt

Elizabeth folded the letter. A smiled played over her lips. It had all been very neatly done, getting Lydia to wed. She wondered who had put such a clever plot together. It was too convoluted for her father and too manipulative for Mr. Darcy. She didn't know Colonel Fitzwilliam, Pratt, Colonel Forster or Mrs. Forster well enough to estimate which of them was likely to have concocted the scheme.

"I take it all is well?" Anne asked, looking up from her book.

"Lydia was rescued from Mr. Wickham and has wed a Mr. Pratt," Elizabeth said.

"Is this Pratt a good man?" Anne asked.

"I don't know much about Mr. Pratt," Elizabeth admitted. She hadn't paid the officers much attention, unlike her younger sisters. "I'm pleased that at least she didn't marry Wickham."

"Pratt was always rather quiet," Kitty said. "He attended parties, but he always seemed to have more duties than the other officers and he didn't dance much. I'm glad Lydia is married. Isn't it lucky there was someone else who loved her so much he was willing to overlook her running away with Mr. Wickham? Why, Pratt must have not danced with her often because he was worshipping her from afar." Kitty let out a sigh, her eyes full of proverbial stars.

Elizabeth exchanged an amused glance with Anne, giving a little shake of her head to indicate she didn't see any reason to disabuse Kitty of her romantic notions.

"Yes," Anne murmured. "It is lucky indeed. Speaking of luck, Elizabeth, could you retrieve the envelope on my writing desk and read what's in it? It pertains to you."

Elizabeth frowned, but went to find the page, returning Lydia's letter to Kitty on her way. She opened the envelope on Anne's desk. Seeing that it was from a bank, she quickly averted her eyes.

"It doesn't pertain to me," Elizabeth said. "Perhaps I should look somewhere else?"

"I think you'll find it does pertain to you," Anne said.

"It's from a bank," Elizabeth said.

"That is correct. Read it."

A brief perusal showed it was indeed from a bank. The salutation was not addressed to Anne, however, but rather to Elizabeth. It was a statement claiming she had three hundred pounds in an account with them.

"I thought we agreed I was staying here as your friend," Elizabeth protested, realizing this was the one hundred pounds a month Anne had offered her, which she'd refused.

"And as your friend, I have given you that," Anne said.

Elizabeth glanced at Kitty, whose eyes were full of curiosity for the exchange. It was clever of Anne to bring up the subject now, in the parlor. She knew Elizabeth wouldn't want to speak too openly with a witness. "I really cannot take this, though it's very kind of you."

"I'm afraid you have no choice," Anne said. "The account is in your name. I have no rights to it."

"What is it?" Kitty asked.

"I wasn't even able to accomplish the task you set me," Elizabeth said, for she hadn't managed to keep Anne from sending most of the staff scurrying away.

"Yes, but you stayed on and put things back together after my mistake."

Footsteps in the hall forestalled Elizabeth's reply. A maid came into the room. "A Mr. Bennet and Mr. Darcy, miss," she said to Anne before bowing and backing away to allow the two to enter.

Elizabeth quickly folded the paper detailing her account and put it in her pocket. She shot a look at Anne that was meant to convey that they would revisit the subject at a later time. She turned back to see Mr. Darcy following her father into the parlor and had to suppress a sigh. Mr. Darcy looked even more handsome than the last time she saw him. Pulling her eyes from his, she hurried to her father.

"Papa," she said, briefly embracing him. "Mr. Darcy," she added with a curtsy.

"Papa," Kitty greeted as she too hugged their father. "Mr. Darcy, how fine to see you again so soon." She curtsied.

Elizabeth hid a smile, taking in the surprise on her father's face.

Kitty hadn't run, or squealed. Her tones were cultured and her curtsy flawless.

"Miss Elizabeth, Miss Kitty," Mr. Darcy said. He bowed. "Mr. Bennet, may I introduce my cousin, Miss de Bourgh."

"You have a splendid home, Miss de Bourgh," Elizabeth's father said. "Thank you for allowing my daughters to stay with you."

Anne didn't stand, but she did smile. "It is I who should thank you, sir, for the loan of them. You are welcome here as well."

"Thank you," her father said. "It's a generous offer, but I shall not trouble you. I have been invited to stay with a Mr. Whitaker."

Out of the corner of her eye, Elizabeth saw Kitty blush.

"Please excuse my manners, but I would be much obliged if I might borrow Elizabeth for a short time? There are some matters of family I must discuss with her," her father continued.

"Of course," Anne said. "Mrs. Allen will be joining us momentarily. Kitty and I shall do quite nicely with her and Mr. Darcy for company. Won't we, Kitty?"

"Yes Miss de Bourgh," Kitty said. Amazingly, her tone wasn't even sullen. She turned to Elizabeth. "You should show Papa where we like to walk. The views are splendid."

"I'll get my bonnet," Elizabeth said. "If you'll excuse me Mr. Darcy, Miss de Bourgh, Kitty. I'll meet you in the foyer, Papa." She dropped a curtsy and hurried away.

Elizabeth hoped no one could tell how much it was affecting her to have Mr. Darcy near. He, of course, looked completely unperturbed, while she was embarrassingly elated to see him again. It wouldn't do for anyone to notice. She all but ran to her room.

After composing herself, Elizabeth met her father in the foyer and led the way outside. Once they were a bit away from the house, he gave her his version of what had transpired in Brighton. It was more detailed and, Elizabeth suspected, a good deal more accurate than Lydia's.

"It was cleverly done," Elizabeth said once he was finished. "Who was the mastermind?"

"In ensuring Wickham boarded that ship, Mr. Darcy," her father said. "In seeing Lydia wed, Pratt."

"Kitty has a very romantic version of what happened."

"And she shall keep it. What I've told you goes no further. Secrets aren't kept by telling more people."

Elizabeth nodded. There was no one she wished to tell. Mr. Darcy already knew the whole of it. "I'm glad that Lydia didn't marry Wickham."

"Pratt will be a much better husband than Wickham would have been," her father agreed.

"You met Mr. Whitaker before coming here?" Elizabeth asked.

Her father nodded. "Mr. Darcy was kind enough to stop there first, though he seemed eager to arrive here." He glanced at her askance.

Elizabeth kept her face composed. "What did you think of Mr. Whitaker?"

"I'm surprised Kitty has caught someone so sensible and eligible. Mrs. Bennet will be delighted."

"Delighted that he's sensible?" she couldn't resist asking.

His eyes smiled but he didn't reply. They walked in silence for a moment. Elizabeth realized they were nearing the spot where she and Mr. Darcy had spoken so intimately and turned them down a different trail. She didn't wish to walk there again unless she could be alone with her memories or beside the man who'd helped create them.

Her mind returned to the discussion she and Anne had been having when her father and Mr. Darcy arrived. She frowned. "I have a problem that I am not sure how to handle," she said.

"You? Have a problem you can't handle?"

"Your implied vote of confidence is noted, but it's true," she said. "When Miss de Bourgh first asked me to stay she offered me a hundred pounds a month. I said I wouldn't take it and she appeared to agree with me. I discovered a short time ago that she's deposited three hundred pounds in a bank account under my name."

"You have been here three months," he said.

"She gave me a piece of paper with the bank's name. She said she couldn't get the money out of the account so she has no way to take it back. She tricked me into getting my signature." Elizabeth spoke that as she realized it, her mind going back to all of the letters Anne had asked her to write, all the signatures she'd signed on page after page of them.

"I fail to see the problem," her father said. "I know you aren't accustomed to the idea of earning money, and I know that you feel it is too much, but she trusted you. Did you ever betray that trust?"

"Of course not."

"If she'd hired a stranger to do what you did, it might have cost her much more than three hundred pounds."

Elizabeth thought about that. Even with Darcy there, a stranger might have taken money from the housekeeping funds. Darcy was too concerned with the farm to pay that much attention to the house and his first choice of housekeeper hadn't turned out well. She didn't even wish to imagine what could have happened if Miss de Bourgh had given an unscrupulous person the same authority she'd bestowed on Elizabeth. "I can see how an untrustworthy person could have done great harm."

"Good. Now, it is my belief that you should be rewarded for what you've done here, so this is what we will do. In a few days, you and Kitty will return home with me."

Elizabeth blinked. Home . . . she did want to go home, didn't she? She missed Jane, and her home. Mr. Darcy had only just returned, though. If she left now, would she ever see him again? She swallowed. Her throat somehow seemed very tight.

"On our way back, we'll stop in London to see the Gardiners," her father was saying.

Elizabeth seized on his words. She needed something to focus on instead of the panic building inside her at the idea of never seeing Mr. Darcy again. Surly, that wouldn't be the case? He must want to see her, and if Darcy wanted something, he would accomplish it.

"You and I will go to the bank together," her father said. "You will

166

withdraw however much money you want to spend. You aren't yet of age but I will make it plain to the bank that it is your money and you can withdraw it as you wish."

"Withdraw? For what?"

"Whatever you like," her father said, casting her a smile. "I must swear you to secrecy, for I can't have your sisters, and especially your mother, knowing about the money Miss de Bourgh has given you. However, you deserve some sort of reward for the work you've done. If you make a purchase on the way home, people will assume the item was a gift from Miss de Bourgh, or that the money used to buy it was."

Elizabeth nodded. "Anything I wish? You mean, a towering pile of novels, or a huge, gaudy, expensive hat?"

Her father eyed her, looking a bit nervous.

"What about an account book for mother?" she asked, making her eyes wide and innocent.

He narrowed his gaze. "Now I know for certain you jest."

"I know," Elizabeth said. "I shall buy my dear sister Lydia a very plain, conservative frock as a wedding gift."

They filled the walk back to the house with talk of possible purchases; frivolous, ridiculous and wise. Elizabeth realized she could get almost as much enjoyment out of imaginary purchases as real ones. She resolved that when it came to it, she wouldn't take out any of the money. It was much more sensible to leave it where it was.

The following day as she was getting ready to leave, Elizabeth bemoaned that she hadn't found a moment to speak quietly with Mr. Darcy. She didn't have anything in mind to talk with him about, but had missed their conversations greatly in his absence. She tried to maintain her typical cheerful demeanor, but she was tormented by the idea of never seeing him again.

Sitting on the edge of her bed, looking around the room she'd spent the last three months in, Elizabeth felt a wave of sorrow. The space looked cold and empty to her, with her things packed away and even then being carried down and loaded into Mr. Whitaker's carriage.

167

She'd hoped, somehow, that Mr. Darcy would offer to take them to London, but there was no reason for him to accompany them and every reason for Mr. Whitaker to.

Elizabeth did want to go home, but she had the feeling it would be strange to be there. She wasn't leaving Rosings quite the same person she'd been when she arrived. She'd never in her life held so many secrets. Darcy's proposal, his role in separating Bingley and Jane, the money she had in the bank, Pratt's manipulation of Lydia; it all seemed like a lot to hold inside.

Trying to shake off her disquiet, she stood and made her way to the foyer, where Anne, Mrs. Allen and Kitty waited.

"Elizabeth," Anne said. "Please do return whenever you like. I shall miss you terribly. Here, take this." She pressed a ten pound note into Elizabeth's hands.

"Thank you," Elizabeth said. She was about to try to return it when she saw the amusement in Anne's eyes. "I shall miss you as well, Miss de Bourgh."

"Farewell, dear," Mrs. Allen said.

"Good bye Mrs. Allen."

"Good by Miss de Bourgh," Kitty said. She flung her arms around Anne with a little sob.

While Anne and Mrs. Allen set about trying to comfort Kitty, the former giving her ten pounds as well, Elizabeth turned to Mr. Darcy.

"Mr. Darcy," she said. "I . . ." She could think of nothing proper to say. I don't want this to be the last time I ever see you, she thought, wishing that somehow he could see it in her eyes.

"Miss Bennet," he said. "It is my hope that we shall meet again before long."

She nodded, curtsying. She didn't want to read overmuch into his statement, but it filled her with hope.

"Papa is waiting, Lizzy," Kitty said, apparently recovered from her surge of grief. "Good bye Mr. Darcy."

"Miss Kitty," he said, bowing to them both.

If Kitty hadn't taken her arm and tugged her away, Elizabeth wasn't sure she would have managed to leave. Then, in a flurry of skirts, they were out the door.

"That was ever so nice of her," Kitty whispered as they headed down the steps. "Now she's given me two-hundred and sixty pounds."

Elizabeth almost tripped, turning startled eyes toward Kitty.

"She gave me two-hundred and fifty as a wedding gift. Isn't that fabulous of her? I love Miss de Bourgh. I've never known anyone so nice."

Before Elizabeth could organize her thoughts, which centered around not feeling as bad for keeping the three hundred pounds if Kitty was to be given nearly as much simply for reading, they were ensconced in Mr. Whitaker's coach. This necessitated a round of greetings between them and their father and Mr. Whitaker, including the necessary polite complements to his conveyance and thankfulness for the use of it. By the time Elizabeth was able to turn away and look back, the door to Rosings was closed.

Chapter Seventeen

Darcy left two weeks after the Bennets, after finally finding a competent housekeeper. The man he assigned to run the farm was one of those who had returned, allowing Darcy to leave it with confidence. Anne had fully recovered and gotten through the three-month period of heavy mourning, which meant other visitors started calling. Anne let it be known she was 'at home' only for a few hours a day. The rest of the time, she spent reading from her increasingly large pile of books.

Anne invited Mrs. Collins to visit two or three times a week, at times there were no other visitors. On the one occasion she invited him, it was obvious Mr. Collins had mixed feelings about that. He was pleased his wife was invited but chagrinned he was not. He consulted with Darcy about it, who suggested that Collins accept it as one of the reasonable eccentricities of a wealthy, yet sheltered spinster heiress.

Although the added and varied company was more pleasant than any of Lady Catherine's guests, Darcy found Rosings unhappily empty without Elizabeth. He returned to Pemberley, where he'd invited Bingley and his unwed sister to join him and Georgiana. That filled his days and evenings in a way that should have been adequate, but Darcy still felt a lack. There was an emptiness in his life where Elizabeth had been, and he often found himself thinking about her when he should be attending to matters at hand.

One matter, an unpleasant one, was telling Georgiana that Wickham had left Britain. He also apprised her that Wickham had tried to disperse the rumor that she'd almost eloped with him, so that she would be ready if anyone was ever crass enough to mention the event. She was very quiet while he spoke and he tried to ignore the tears in her eyes. Of Wickham's failed attempt to run off with Mrs. Pratt, he said nothing.

That accomplished, Darcy tasked himself with trying to deduce whether or not Bingley still had feelings for Jane Bennet. At first, he thought that since Bingley never spoke of her, he must have recovered from his infatuation. After a few days, however, it occurred to Darcy that there was a pointedness to Bingley's silence on the subject. He never talked of his time in Hertfordshire, but mentioned every other place he had lived for the past three years. He also made no mention of a wonderful woman he'd just met, which was unusual for him. By the time Bingley and his sister left for their next engagement, Darcy still had no answer.

There were many times during Bingley's stay that Darcy was on the verge of bringing up Miss Jane Bennet. He permitted his friend to leave without doing so, however. He still worried that if he broached the idea it would be tantamount to telling Bingley to marry Miss Bennet.

Life returned to normal for Darcy, except that it couldn't be. Normal was now strange feeling. Even in his beloved Pemberley with his sister there, the world was an empty place without Elizabeth.

Almost two months after he'd last seen her, Darcy sat at his desk trying to read over his mail. It contained a number of business letters he knew he should focus on, but he worked with less alacrity than usual, his mind often straying to Elizabeth. He wondered what she was doing. Did she miss him? It had been two months. What if she had met a gentleman she cared for?

Darcy scowled at the thought, forcing himself to see to his affairs. He had no right to wonder if Elizabeth Bennet had met a gentleman. Until he asked for her hand again and was accepted, he had no right to concern over her activities. Yet how could he ask if he couldn't see her? He looked at the ledgers open on his desk. Did he have no business that would take him to Hertfordshire?

In truth, Darcy could travel to Hertfordshire whenever he wished, of course, and knew why he did not. Mr. Bennet would certainly invite him to stay in his house if he knew Darcy wanted to be there. If he went with no excuse, it was tantamount to proposing. He needed to see Elizabeth again, to assess if her 'I don't know' had changed to something more positive. He wouldn't be able to stand the pain of handing his heart to her a second time and being rejected.

Unable to focus on them, Darcy set aside his ledgers and letters of business and opened the first of his personal correspondence. It was from Anne. She said that the harvest looked as if it would go well and that she had invited Miss Mary Bennet to stay with her. If she'd invited Elizabeth back, he'd been prepared to take it as a sign. He would have ridden to Rosings and reissued his proposal.

She'd invited Miss Mary, however. Well, Darcy hoped his cousin could improve Miss Mary as much as she'd improved Miss Kitty. He eyed the next letter on the pile.

It was from Bingley. Never before had letters from his closest friend given Darcy pause. Ever since Elizabeth's vehement assertion that her sister did love Bingley, Darcy felt a shadow of guilt when dealing with the man. It weighed on what had once been a very cordial friendship.

Grimacing, Darcy opened the letter. It was an invitation for Darcy to join Bingley for shooting in Netherfield as soon as he wished to come. Darcy reread the line twice. What was Bingley doing, returning to Netherfield? Either he was so indifferent to Miss Bennet that he didn't consider her, or he cared for her deeply enough to ignore Darcy's advice.

Darcy was out of his chair before he knew it. "Stevens," he called and he strolled from his office. He turned to the footman waiting outside. "Send Stevens to my quarters. We've packing to see to. Have a carriage brought round. Tell Alderson we're off to Netherfield."

"Yes, sir," the man said, hurrying away.

Darcy didn't waste a moment. He was tired of living with the guilt of not knowing if he'd wronged his best friend and he was miserable without Elizabeth. He wasn't sure what he meant to do about either, but he knew he wouldn't find the answers in Pemberley. Not when

Bingley and Elizabeth were both in Hertfordshire. If he'd wanted a sign, surely Bingley's letter was one.

When he reached Netherfield, he could tell Bingley was surprised to see him so soon. In fact, he arrived just a few hours after Bingley had. Ever amiable, Bingley took his precipitous entrance in stride. To Darcy's surprise and relief, Miss Bingley was not in attendance. Apparently, she'd stuck to her declaration to never return. It would be relaxing to be with Bingley and not have to walk the tightrope of being pleasant to his sister without encouraging her to think he had the slightest interest in her.

The following day, Darcy and Bingley rode out to scout possible hunting locations and examine the property. They spoke little except about the purported purpose of the ride, and Darcy mourned their loss of easy comradery. He knew the tension between them stemmed from his guilt and whatever it was Bingley had planned for his visit to Hertfordshire. In spite of that, they still spent a pleasant enough day, riding for several hours.

They'd only just finished a light meal after returning when they had their first caller, Sir William Lucas. Sir William was the father of Elizabeth's friend, Mrs. Collins, so Darcy did not mind the intrusion as much as he might have. William might mention Elizabeth, after all. He and Bingley stood as the man was shown into the parlor.

"Mr. Bingley, Mr. Darcy, it's so good to see you both back in Netherfield," Sir William said, bowing. His tone conveyed what seemed to be genuine pleasure. He had always been friendly before, but there was more in this greeting.

"We're pleased to be back," Bingley said. "Please sit. I, for one, missed the fine company and country air Hertfordshire has to offer."

He didn't look at Darcy as he said it, but Darcy had the distinct impression the remark was aimed at him.

"Very kind of you to say as much." Sir William beamed at Bingley. "Mr. Darcy, my condolences on your aunt and might I add, my daughter, Mrs. Collins, spoke very highly of the unflagging assistance you

174

extended to Miss de Bourgh when Lady Catherine died. She said you were willing to do any job, no matter how large or small, to keep Rosings running smoothly."

"I did what had to be done," Darcy said, a bit surprised by the praise. He couldn't see how his shoveling manure was a particular virtue. He didn't want the cows to be milked in stalls that weren't cleaned or the horses to stand in filth.

"Just as you did what had to be done when you rescued poor Mrs. Pratt from that villain Wickham?"

"When I did what?" Darcy asked, shocked. If anything, he'd been prepared for veiled comments about Georgiana's elopement and had been almost eager for the chance to correct any rumors. He hadn't expected mention of Mrs. Pratt.

"Come now, all the world knows of it," Sir William said. He leaned forward. "How Mr. Wickham fled the country to avoid debtor's prison. How he first tried to run off with Miss Lydia to get her dowry for paying his debts." He spoke in a low voice completely at odds with his assertion that everyone already knew.

"I think it would be best if we didn't belabor the subject," Darcy said.

"What subject?" Bingley was all eagerness. "Come, Darcy, you've said nothing of this. What's happened?"

Darcy shook his head, frowning. "It's exaggeration."

"Now, don't be modest," Sir William said. He turned back to Bingley. "I have it from the girl's own mother that Mr. Darcy and Mr. Pratt rode at a gallop in the dark of night for hours and rescued the fair maiden. Wickham kidnapped her, you know, for her dowry, knowing that her father and uncle would pay him more than her share, because she is her mother's favorite."

Darcy grimaced. Not only were the details wrong, he wasn't even certain if the word maiden applied. Not that he would ever correct that. If he said that Mrs. Pratt had gone willingly, he would cast a slur on her name that she might never live down. The fact that the slur was earned didn't matter.

"Come now, Darcy, let's have the lot of it," Bingley said, obviously enjoying himself.

Darcy shook his head. "I did little."

"He's a local hero," Sir William said. "I would be honored if you'd dine with us soon."

"We would be happy to, sir," Bingley said. "Send round a time and date."

"I will, I will," Sir William said. He stood and Darcy and Bingley followed suit. "Wanted to be the first to see you again, Mr. Darcy, Mr. Bingley. Glad you've returned."

They exchanged bows and a footman showed Sir William out. As soon as he was gone, Bingley turned to Darcy. "Well?"

"I, along with several others including her father, assisted Mrs. Pratt," Darcy said. "We did put Wickham aboard a ship to Spain. There's really nothing more to it."

Bingley eyed him for a moment, looking disappointed. "If you say so. I know better than to try to change your mind on a subject."

Did Darcy imagine the vindictive edge to that statement? Again, he wondered why Bingley had returned to Netherfield and if it had to do with Miss Jane Bennet. Had he invited Darcy for the purpose of proving him wrong?

Bingley continued to scrutinize him, but Darcy shook his head, pressing his lips closed in a firm line. He refused to divulge any further information about Mrs. Pratt. He trusted Bingley, but it wouldn't do to ever have Lydia Pratt's actions come to light. Bingley was a terrible liar, especially to those who knew him. Words aside, a guilty look in response to probing by his sisters was all it would take to put their tongues wagging and a different story would reach the world.

"If we're not to speak of that obviously delicate subject, I suggest we speak of another," Bingley said. He regarded Darcy with determined eyes. "I brought you here for a reason. I cannot get Miss Bennet out of my mind. I know you said before that you didn't think she loved me, but

176

I love her. I want to meet her again and decide if I love her enough to marry her without her loving me. You said you thought she enjoyed my company. Could she like me enough to be happy with me? I have to see her again." This last, Bingley said with a note of desperation in his tone.

Darcy recognized that emotion. It lurked in his own breast. "Why do you want me here?"

"Because if you are looking over my shoulder I will be more careful. I have a tendency to rush headlong into things. Even if you don't say anything, knowing you're watching me will make me more careful. In spite of how much I care for Miss Bennet, I don't know if I can marry a woman who doesn't love me. I'm afraid I'll propose before I can answer that question for myself."

"If you want someone to make sure you don't propose to Miss Bennet, why not one or both of your sisters?" They'd made no secret of not approving of Jane Bennet and had done a skillful job of preventing a proposal thus far.

"Because you want me to be happy. My sisters want me to be rich and well connected," Bingley said bitterly.

"I do want you to be happy. Remember that," Darcy said, realizing it was time to tell Bingley the truth. "There are some things I'm going to tell you that will probably make you angry with me."

Bingley looked at him with puzzled expectancy. "This sounds serious. Should I sit back down?"

"You may want to," Darcy said, but they both remained standing. "First, Miss Bennet was in London for most of the winter. She called on your sisters who cut the acquaintance. I suspect that Miss Bingley told Miss Bennet you knew she was in London."

"Miss Bennet must have thought I was avoiding her. She will never forgive me." Bingley groaned, sinking into a chair.

"Miss Bennet is a generous hearted woman who tends to think the best of people, but she isn't stupid. I suspect she knows the truth."

"Still..."

"Still, she has reason to be angry with you. The whole

177

neighborhood was expecting you to propose last year. Instead, you left. Think how that looked to everyone."

Bingley leaned back in his chair, looking up at Darcy. "I'm only a little angry with you. I know you thought she didn't love me. You always look out for me."

"There's more," Darcy said, taking the chair opposite Bingley. "I found out last April that Miss Elizabeth believes that Miss Bennet loved you."

"What! And you didn't tell me?"

"If you were willing to go five months without any attempt to see her, I had to believe you didn't love her," Darcy said.

"I do love her. I'm sure I do. It's been nearly a year and I still think of her constantly. I went along with you because I knew you were right. I fall in love too easily. This is different, though, Darcy. This is something more."

Darcy nodded. "It seems to be."

"Do you think, after all I've put her through, Jane still loves me?"

"I don't know," Darcy said, shaking his head. "You must discover that for yourself, I think."

Bingley surged to his feet. "I'm calling on the Bennets. Will you join me?"

It bordered on being late to make a call, but they went. As soon as they were shown into the parlor, Darcy realized the tone of the family had changed with the two youngest daughters married and the middle one staying with Anne. The only silly one left was Mrs. Bennet, and her silliness wasn't as evident in the company of her husband and two oldest daughters.

"Mr. Darcy," Mrs. Bennet cried, rushing over to him. "How good to see you. Ever since I learned what you did for Lydia I've wanted to thank you. And you helped Kitty too! And now Mary is there and she is meeting all sorts of eligible men. How can I thank you?"

"Miss de Bourgh is the one who invited Miss Mary and Mrs. Whitaker," Darcy protested, taken aback by both her friendliness and praise.

He looked past her, meeting Elizabeth's amused gaze. He offered her a smile, which she returned immediately. Something inside him relaxed, falling back into place after long months of being maligned.

"You just missed Sir William, who called to tell us how humble you are. That's your real fault, you know. You don't appreciate how good you are. You should be proud of yourself, but you are too modest. I was always suspicious of Wickham, but everyone accepted his lies about you. As I keep telling my sister, Wickham was not to be trusted. I always knew as much. Oh, hello, Mr. Bingley. It's nice to see you too."

"How is Mrs. Pratt?" Darcy asked, attempting to turn the topic away from his supposed character flaw of not enough pride.

"Quite well indeed," Mrs. Bennet said. "It's wonderful my dear sweet Lydia found a man who loves her so devotedly. Captain Pratt is a terribly fine young man."

Darcy nodded. He was in no way convinced that Pratt loved his wife, but it would be the height of ill manners to disagree.

"Though, do you know, poor thing, Captain Pratt said she may only have two new bonnets a year," Mrs. Bennet continued. "Two! Why, he's a captain. Surely he can afford three times as many bonnets as that for my Lydia. I can't imagine what the man is thinking. She's quite cross about it."

"I'm sure he's only being conservative now so that he can buy her something even better than bonnets in the future, Mama," Elizabeth said.

Like food, Darcy thought.

"Do you know what?" Mrs. Bennet asked, lowering her voice in a conspiratorial fashion. "You may well be right, Lizzy. It's still early, but Lydia is certain she's already with child. Trust my Lydia to be such a good wife that she gets with child on her wedding night."

"Mama," Elizabeth said in a reprimanding tone, shooting an embarrassed look at Darcy.

He coughed into his hand, hoping the news wasn't true. If Mrs.

Pratt gave birth too soon after her wedding day, it would only add fuel to rumors he'd worked to suppress. "And what of Mrs. Whitaker?" he asked.

"Kitty is doing well, of course," Mrs. Bennet said. "Not as well as Lydia, but well enough for any mama to be pleased. Mr. Whitaker was so good to take her. Such a nice young gentleman. I don't know how my Kitty managed it."

"She is enjoying Kent, I hope?" Darcy asked.

"She must be. She writes me terrible drivel about the birds and flowers there. On and on about flowers. She sneezes so much, you wouldn't think she could tolerate the things."

"Flowers?" he said. He exchanged a glance with Elizabeth, recalling how Mrs. Whitaker had railed against having to learn of flowers.

"Yes, indeed. Let me see." Mrs. Bennet patted about herself, eventually coming up with a much-folded letter. "I'll read it to you. *Mama, I must tell you of how my dear Harold proposed. You see, he knew what Miss de Bourgh had been making me read, so he came one day and didn't ask for me to walk, but instead to see me in the parlor. Well, I waited there, all aflutter you know, and in he came with an armful of the most beautiful roses. Knowing what Miss de Bourgh's book said about roses, that they mean love, I couldn't contain myself Mama. Before he could even ask, I jumped up and cried 'yes!' and do you know what he did? He rushed over and kissed me right there, in front of Miss de Bourgh and a maid, and I didn't care one bit, although we did crush some of the roses. I didn't even mind that the thorns drew a bit of blood from both of us, although the stain never came out of my dress. Miss de Bourgh said that some people have sworn blood oaths and our engagement was a blood oath. I dried and pressed some of the roses. Oh Mama, I'm going to fill our home with roses as long as they are blooming and never forget that moment.* And she sent this with it," Mrs. Bennet added, holding up a paper-thin pressed cluster of rose petals.

Her voice had grown a bit tattered as she read and Darcy could see tears in her eyes. She carefully folded the pressed petals back into the

180

note and put it away, taking out her kerchief. Elizabeth patted her on the shoulder.

Taking in Elizabeth's face, Darcy realized it was the first time he'd seen her look on her mother with such tender sentiment. Usually, Elizabeth looked exasperated, embarrassed or amused by her mother, but this look was the loving look of a child for her parents. He glanced away. He, who hadn't known the love of parents in many years, felt a twinge of jealousy. It occurred to him that, though she was often deserving of Elizabeth's typical looks, there was much to be said for having a mother who loved you.

"My apologies, Mr. Darcy," Mrs. Bennet said, tucking her handkerchief away. "I don't know what came over me." She glanced over his shoulder, where Jane Bennet and Bingley sat whispering. "A mother does so want to see all of her daughters happy."

"As is only natural," Darcy said.

Mrs. Bennet's face grew contemplative. "May I ask why you and Mr. Bingley have returned to Hertfordshire, Mr. Darcy?"

"Mama," Elizabeth said.

"We've come for some fall sport," Darcy said. He did enjoy hunting, so it wasn't completely untrue. Elizabeth seemed pleased enough to see him, though, that he was starting to think he wouldn't need an excuse for being there. He would offer for her, and she would say yes. Of course, that's what he'd thought the first time he'd asked, so he didn't dare be too confident.

"Have you had any luck?"

"We haven't had the chance to hunt yet," Darcy said. "We rode out today to select possible locations, but that is all."

"Well then, Mr. Darcy, I think you and Mr. Bingley ought to stay for supper," Mrs. Bennet said.

"We wouldn't wish to impose," Darcy said. "It's already late for us to call on you, for which I apologize."

"Nonsense," Mrs. Bennet said. "It would be no imposition at all. I understand neither of you brought your sisters with you, and you've

181

shot nothing yet. Why, you'll go back to such a quiet, empty home and no birds for your table. You simply must dine with us instead, mustn't he, Lizzy?"

"Do please stay to dine with us if you like, Mr. Darcy," Elizabeth said. "It really wouldn't be an imposition. I'm sure my father would welcome other gentlemen to converse with."

"I am not as overwhelmed as I was with five daughters at home," Mr. Bennet said, "but I am still outnumbered."

Elizabeth's face persuaded Darcy. When she looked at him like that, as if she really did want him to stay, Darcy couldn't say no. He glanced over his shoulder to find Bingley still speaking quietly with Jane Bennet, their heads close together and giving every appearance that they'd forgotten any other people existed. "We would be pleased to share your table. Thank you."

"Jane," Mrs. Bennet said. Jane looked startled at being spoken to. "There's a painting in the hall that Mr. Bingley hasn't seen."

"A painting?" Jane asked, completely puzzled.

"Yes, the one with birds. Since he's here to hunt and hasn't seen any birds yet, maybe he should look at some in the painting."

To remind him what a bird looked like? Darcy thought, amused.

"There is another painting in the library that has birds in it. Maybe he'd like to see that one too."

Elizabeth mouthed the word 'one' to Darcy, holding up a single finger. She then held her thumb and finger less than an inch apart and mouthed a single word he didn't catch.

Bingley and Miss Bennet rose to go into the hall. As they were leaving, Darcy said to Bingley, "We're staying for dinner."

"We are? That's good," Bingley said as they left.

"I have to talk to the cook about dinner, with two unexpected guests," Mrs. Bennet said, standing. Instead of leaving, she moved nearer to him. "You must think me terrible, Mr. Darcy, but Mr. Bingley simply must propose this time. My poor Jane was nearly undone when he left. It will break her heart if he does so again, and I won't stand for it. You've been so good to our family, surely you must understand."

There was a fierceness in her gaze that took Darcy aback. He contented himself with a nod and she smiled, stepping out to the hallway, obviously trying to listen. Her look became intent and she held a finger to her lips, though he hadn't given any indication he intended to speak.

"I really have to talk to the cook about dinner," she finally said, looking back into the room. "Besides, they are only talking about the painting," she added in a lower voice.

After Mrs. Bennet left, Darcy asked Elizabeth, "What were you trying to tell me?"

She looked a bit embarrassed.

"You were trying to communicate secretly? What were you saying?" Mr. Bennet asked, raising his eyebrows.

She repeated her actions and said, "One."

"I caught that," Darcy said. "What I don't understand is the second part."

"Small," she said, smiling. "It's an exaggeration to say that the library holds a painting with birds. There's one with one small bird."

"It's a hummingbird," Mr. Bennet said. "I don't think it pertains much to hunting."

Darcy nodded his understanding and the conversation turned to hunting until Mrs. Bennet returned. Darcy wouldn't have supposed it earlier in the day, but he enjoyed dinner. He didn't even mind that Mrs. Bennet was silly. With everyone else being sensible, good conversation flourished.

The one shadow on the meal was Jane Bennet. He now had both Elizabeth's and her mother's assurance that Jane Bennet loved Bingley, but he still couldn't tell. Darcy realized he might have to admit to himself that he simply couldn't read her expression as one might most women's.

If Jane Bennet's feelings for Bingley weren't clear, Bingley's feelings for her were. Darcy was sure Bingley left dinner even more in love than ever. He wasn't sure what Bingley should do about it, though.

Before departing, Mrs. Bennet suggested they all walk together the following day. Her blatant attempt to keep Jane Bennet and Bingley together caused Elizabeth to look embarrassed, but Bingley agreed eagerly. Darcy was equally willing to return but he preferred to think he had the decorum not to permit his enthusiasm to show.

Chapter Eighteen

Elizabeth sat at the pianoforte attempting to practice. It was difficult, of course, as she kept looking over her shoulder out the window. Mr. Darcy and Mr. Bingley were due to arrive any moment to escort her and Jane on a walk.

She'd tried for months to convince herself that it didn't matter if she never saw Mr. Darcy again. Much as she'd longed to see him and had been sure there was a connection between them, theirs had been a somewhat tumultuous relationship. What manner of man would be able to look past her continued disagreement with him on the point of Bingley and Jane, and her harsh, regrettably, vehement refusal of a proposal of marriage? She worried he wouldn't ever return to Hertfordshire. Yet, that last day they'd walked together in Kent, he'd seemed as if he cared.

Then word came that he was there, at Netherfield. What was more, no sooner had Sir William left, after imparting the news of Mr. Darcy's arrival, then he should show up at their door. With Mr. Bingley in tow, no less, and both of them in seeming accord and intent on seeing her and Jane. Mr. Darcy had even asked after her sisters and been polite to her mother. It could mean but one thing; he still wished to wed her.

Her fingers stumbled over the keys, trembling at the thought of him asking again.

"Elizabeth, do cease that racket," her mother said. "Did you not practice once in Kent? How abysmal your playing has become, when I once liked it so well."

"I'm sorry, Mama," Elizabeth said. She glanced at Jane, who sat stitching with apparent content. How could Jane be so calm? Her sister looked up at her and smiled, as if guessing Elizabeth's thoughts.

"Is that someone at the door?" Mrs. Bennet said, peering past her out the window.

Elizabeth swiveled on the bench. Outside, Mr. Darcy glanced up, catching her eye and smiling before turning his attention to the door she could hear opening in the foyer. Elizabeth exerted all of her self-control to stay seated.

"A Mr. Darcy and a Mr. Bingley are here to collect Miss Jane and Miss Elizabeth for a walk," their maid said as she reached the parlor door.

Elizabeth's mother looked between her and Jane. "Well, off with you both. Enjoy yourselves."

Elizabeth jumped to her feet, taking up her shawl. "Yes, Mama," she said, giving her mother a kiss on the cheek as she passed.

"Yes, Mama," Jane said, following.

Together, they hurried to the front door and out to greet Mr. Darcy and Mr. Bingley. They immediately set off, the four of them walking together. By the time they were out of sight from the house, they'd paired off into two couples.

Elizabeth walked beside Mr. Darcy, stealing glances at him. It was a fine early autumn day, with a startlingly blue sky and pleasantly brisk air. They strolled through the scenic Hertfordshire countryside, bright with fall color. Ahead of them, Jane and Mr. Bingley walked with arms brushing, speaking in voices too low to hear. Elizabeth slowed her pace even further and Darcy adjusted his. Soon, Jane and Bingley could hardly be seen.

When Jane and Mr. Bingley were out of earshot, Elizabeth decided she had to ask Mr. Darcy about them. If he'd come to see her for the reason she hoped, she needed to know what had transpired before she could give her answer with complete confidence. "Did you bring it up or did Mr. Bingley?"

"I would like to pretend to misunderstand you, but I'm afraid you would only clarify," Darcy said with a wry smile. "No, I didn't have a change of heart. I did not tell Bingley about what you said until after we came here. He decided on his own that he still loves her and wanted to come here to reconsider proposing."

"I see," Elizabeth said, relief filling her. The feeling was strong enough to make her reconsider her previous position, reflecting on Mr. Darcy's stance. While he'd been terribly wrong in separating Jane and Bingley and in continuing to keep them apart, her response to the news that Bingley had returned of his own volition couldn't be ignored. Mr. Darcy was right. Once the initial period of separation had ended, Bingley had to decide to return unprompted. She didn't want Jane with anyone who didn't love her enough to pursue that love.

"As he is my friend and I wish to see him happy, I must ask, does she still love him?"

Elizabeth turned to him with raised brows. Asking that was tantamount to declaring that he now believed her that Jane had, at one time, love Mr. Bingley. It was almost an apology, in a way. As such, she felt she must reply with the truth. "I'm not sure. She did when he left. She's been sad, but she conceals it well and won't speak about it. I don't know if she was sad because she lost Mr. Bingley or because she lost his character."

"His character is fine. He thought he was doing what was right for both of them."

"I don't think he was," Elizabeth said slowly. "In fairness, I am not certain."

"If they marry now, will the ten months of separation be a bad thing? I'm assuming she forgives him."

"If she agrees to marry him, she will have," Elizabeth said confidently. "You must know Jane well enough to see she isn't a woman who would wield a slight as a marital weapon. She is the very soul of forgiveness."

"Speaking about forgiveness, you were justifiably angry with me last April. I completely misunderstood you. I apologized earlier for insulting your family, but I didn't realize that I'd insulted you as well. I hope you can forgive me for that."

"Easily. I think we've both learned a lot since then," she said. Should she tell him that she'd learned he wasn't full of arrogance and pride, or that she wasn't sure she could endure another two months without him?

He stopped walking. Elizabeth turned to face him. She found she was almost holding her breath.

"I also mentioned change of heart. I want to make it clear to you that my heart has not changed," Darcy said.

"Mine has, since last fall. It's changed very much." She searched his face, willing him to ask.

"You know how much I care for you," Darcy said. "Elizabeth Bennet, will you marry me?"

She paused. Not because she wanted to increase the suspense, nor because she was uncertain of her answer. She wanted to chide him for putting his principles above their happiness. If he'd only mentioned her thoughts on Jane to Bingley months ago and put her greatest grievance to rest . . . and yet, she would love him less if he didn't have those principles. "I will," she said. "Gladly."

She stepped forward into his embrace, as she'd longed to do. When their lips met, his kiss was everything she'd dreamed it would be, but so much better for being real.

Chapter Nineteen

Logic told Darcy not to expect any difficulty in getting Mr. Bennet's permission to marry Elizabeth, but he was filled with relief when Mr. Bennet said, "Yes, of course you have my permission. I'm glad to see such long-standing affection in a suitor for my daughter's hand. Kitty and Lydia both wed quickly enough to make a father's heart uneasy."

"Long standing affection?" Darcy repeated. Had Elizabeth told her father about his failed attempt to court her?

"I agree that Lizzy is wonderful, but you aren't going to tell me you fell in love with her in the less than twenty-four hours since you called yesterday. I can only assume your affection is born of your time together at Rosings."

"Staying at Rosings helped," Darcy admitted, glad Mr. Bennet didn't know of his humiliating first proposal. Besides, there was another issue they must discuss. "As I shall now frequent Hertfordshire, I must ask what people are saying about me? Sir William thinks I'm a hero and I've never seen Mrs. Bennet so welcoming."

"I think the gist of it is that you knew Wickham's character was bad, but you refused to tell the world about him in the hopes that he'd reformed. You also didn't think it was fair to use the weight of your wealth and position to give a bad name to the man who was your father's favorite." Mr. Bennet grinned, his clear enjoyment in telling the story giving Darcy a fair guess as to who put out that interpretation of events. "When you discovered that Lydia was in danger of being abducted, you got on your horse and rode across country to rescue her. You discovered Mr. Pratt was her one true love, and the two of you rescued her. Wickham left the country to die on a foreign battlefield to avoid fighting a duel with you."

"I discovered Miss Lydia was in danger because she wrote her sister that she was eloping. If she was eloping, she wasn't abducted," Darcy protested. "This all also ignores the facts that there were four of us in the rescue and most of the trip was by coach."

"Ah, but your modesty and natural reserve keep you from giving all the details."

"I don't care for the idea of letting a lie stand, but the details would harm Mrs. Pratt. Neither you, your wife and daughters, or Captain Pratt deserve that."

"I agree," Mr. Bennet said, his smile broadening. "It seems you must let the story stand. Don't worry overmuch. Everyone knows they don't have the whole story. It pleases them to make you a hero."

"I don't want to be a hero, especially not for something I didn't really do," Darcy said.

"That, as well as what you actually did, makes me think you deserving of the label," Mr. Bennet said with more seriousness than he'd yet shown. "You and Elizabeth will never live here, only visit. Hopefully it won't bother you excessively to keep silent on the matter."

Darcy nodded and they moved on to the happier subject of details about his upcoming wedding.

In spite of his reluctant acceptance of what Mr. Bennet had done concerning his reputation, Darcy found the time he spent in Hertfordshire a trial. He'd been deferred to in the past because of his wealth and connections, but this was the first time he'd ever been treated as a hero. He found it disconcerting, and not simply because it seemed to make him more approachable. It stirred guilt inside him, to be given credit for something he hadn't accomplished.

"It's not a sensation I'm accustomed to or comfortable with," he said to Elizabeth one day, after attempting to explain how he felt. It had been more than a week since his proposal, and there were still two Sundays before they could wed. They were on what had become their daily walk, trailing well behind Bingley and Jane. "I have no notion what to do regarding it, however."

"I'm afraid you shall simply have to accept it," she said, smiling up at him. "The honor and principles which invoke such guilt in you will never allow you to gainsay the rumors."

"I've never expended so much effort worrying over a rumor," he said, shaking his head.

"Exactly, so why begin now? If you never troubled yourself to care about or correct uncomplimentary rumors, why worry over one that praises you? Look at it as restoring balance."

He narrowed his eyes. He wouldn't call being labeled a hero balance.

"As I see it, you should ignore all rumors, good or bad," she continued.

A slight vehemence in her tone gave him pause. "We aren't still speaking of the rumor that I'm a hero, are we?"

"In a way we are." Her smile turned wry. "The new rumor is that you shall toss me over for Jane. Popular opinion says you should be rewarded by marrying her. She is prettier and much nicer than I am. She should be your reward."

He stopped walking and caught her hand, pulling her around to face him. With a quick glance to make sure Bingley and Jane Bennet were well ahead of them and still walking, Darcy pulled Elizabeth into his arms. "There is no one prettier than you," he said, leaning close to whisper the words in her ear.

She shivered slightly and turned her head so their lips almost met. "No one? I think perhaps you exaggerate."

"No one to me," he said, silencing any further protest on her part with a kiss.

When they resumed walking, she glanced askance at him, her smile back in place. "So I may assume you don't wish to wed Jane." This time, her tone held only amusement.

"I admire your sister, but I don't want to marry her."

"That's good," she said. "I would hate to be jealous of Jane."

"More important considerations aside, Bingley would never forgive me if I married your sister," he added.

"Is he planning to do anything about his attraction to her, or is he going to stay long enough to raise her hopes and then leave her?" Elizabeth asked with a bit of asperity in her voice.

"Bingley is taking his time. He wants to be certain."

"His uncertainty is making me nervous," she said. "I never sympathized with my mother's claim that her nerves bother her, but my concern for Jane casts a pall over what should be the happiest time in my life."

"Truly?" He asked. He didn't like the idea of a pall, but he was irrationally pleased to hear her call their days together the happiest time in her life.

"Some." She glanced at him again. "I must admit, I've come into partial agreement with your point of view. In one thing especially you were completely correct; if he doesn't love Jane enough to take the step, perhaps they shouldn't marry."

"I'll talk to him," Darcy said. As the words left his mouth, it occurred to him that his heart was now completely hers. In spite of months of refusing to say anything that might unfairly influence Bingley to propose to Jane Bennet, he'd offered almost eagerly. He realized he would do most anything to spare Elizabeth pain.

"No, you were right about that as well," she said. She made a face, as if she couldn't believe her own words. "You shouldn't push him into a marriage he doesn't really want."

"Does your sister love him?"

"Yes," she said. "I've been observing her carefully for the last few days, and I believe she does. I think it's even more difficult to tell than before because Jane is afraid to open herself to heartbreak again, uncertain if he returns her sentiment."

Darcy nodded, resolved to speak to Bingley when the chance next presented itself. He wouldn't be pushing, but rather fulfilling the role Bingley had asked him to there to take. Someone had to end the absurdity of Bingley waiting to propose until he knew that Jane Bennet loved him, and Miss Bennet waiting to show her feelings until she knew her heart wouldn't be broken again. The way the two of them were, they would never manage to be happy. "Do you know what I think?" he asked, taking Elizabeth's hand in his.

"I most assuredly do not," she replied.

"I think we should spend less time speaking of other people's affections and more time practicing our own." With that, he pulled her into his arms once again.

The following morning found Darcy and Bingley eating breakfast alone, as was typical. Impatient to broach the subject of Miss Jane Bennet, Darcy waited only until they'd served themselves from the sideboard and sat. "You asked me to come with you to look over your shoulder. I've done so," he said.

"Considering your engagement to Miss Elizabeth, that's not all you've done," Bingley said. "I wonder if that's the real reason you came."

His tone had a touch of annoyance that Darcy didn't normally associate with the cheerful Mr. Bingley. "I came for both reasons," Darcy said.

"Your engagement contradicts some of your former arguments against Jane."

Yes, Bingley was definitely cross with him. "Your sisters argued against her family. I was more concerned that she didn't appear to love you."

"You spoke of her family."

"I did," Darcy allowed. "I said that you should take into consideration that they would be an embarrassment to you, but with the two youngest sisters now married, that is less of a problem. I also expressed concern that you might have to support Mrs. Bennet and any unwed sisters when Mr. Bennet eventually passes. Since Elizabeth is marrying someone clearly able to support Mrs. Bennet and her remaining two unmarried daughters, that is no longer an obstacle to marriage."

"Two unmarried daughters?" Bingley asked.

"Mary and Jane," Darcy said. "Of course, I'll never be required to support Jane. She's attractive enough that when she decides to wed, she will have plenty of choices. She may not be able to marry a gentleman, but there are merchants and attorneys who would be delighted to have a beautiful wife who is the daughter of one."

"Merchants and attorneys?" Bingley's voice rose in volume and agitation.

"Well, she lives in a rather restricted society. However, once Elizabeth and I are married, we'll certainly invite her to Pemberley. I also feel she should join Elizabeth when we go to London this winter. There are quite a number of men who would be delighted to marry someone with her beauty and temperament. You are correct. There's no reason to relegate her to merchants and attorneys before bringing her to London for a season or two."

"London?" Bingley bit out, glaring across the table.

"It's for the best. I don't think Miss Bennet will be content to be a burden to her family. If given the opportunity, she'll find a husband she can tolerate. Of course, Elizabeth thinks Jane loves you. I thought you loved her, as you said, but you don't seem to be eager to do anything about it, so I can only assume you've had a change of heart. In that case, and as she's my future sister, I must ask you not to toy with the lady's affections any longer."

"Toy with her affections?" Bingley sputtered. "I love her."

Darcy lifted his cup to take a sip of coffee, regarding Bingley over the rim. He set it down, unable to keep his amusement from his face any longer.

Bingley pushed back his chair, his food untouched. "Is it too early to call?"

"It would be better to wait until she's awake," Darcy said.

194

Chapter Twenty

Elizabeth sat down to dinner with her parents, Jane, Mr. Darcy and Mr. Bingley. It was a celebratory occasion, and one which lightened her heart considerably. That morning, just as they'd finished breakfast, Mr. Bingley had marched up to their front door and demanded to see Jane. Before the plates had been cleared from the table, the two were engaged.

"Two daughters wed and two soon to be," Elizabeth's mother cried as she took her place at the foot of the table. "Nothing will ever rival my happiness. Remember this, Mr. Bennet. Remember I said it. Nothing could ever be so pleasing as this."

"Oh Mama," Jane said, shaking her head.

"Don't worry, my dear," Elizabeth's father said. "I shall endeavor to recall these words of yours with the sureness I apply to recalling all of your utterances."

"Mr. Bennet, you torment me so," her mother wailed. "With guests to witness it. My future sons, no less! What a terrible man you are, Mr. Bennet."

"I daresay I am," Elizabeth's father said, applying himself to his meal.

"Mr. Bingley, Mr. Darcy," her mother said. "Did I tell you that Mary wrote? It seems Miss de Bourgh is paying her fifty pounds every month! Fifty pounds! Mary says she is trying to please Miss de Bourgh by reading a variety of books. She finds them very enlightening." Her mother took out the letter. "She wrote, that *Reading makes a full man; conference a ready man; and writing an exact man.* Isn't that clever of her?"

Elizabeth exchanged an amused glance with Darcy, glad to see he also recognized the quotation. At least Mary's views were being expanded. She didn't doubt Anne's willpower, but she wasn't sure there would be as much success in Mary's case as there had been in Kitty's.

Her mother continued to expound on how wonderful Miss de Bourgh was. Elizabeth and Jane spent a good deal of time talking with her so that their father could carry on an intelligent conversation with Mr. Darcy and Mr. Bingley. Elizabeth hoped their future husbands appreciated what she and Jane were doing.

Near the end of the meal, her mother went silent, taking in the three men speaking quietly together at the other end of the table. "But look at me, speaking endlessly of Miss de Bourgh when the truly wonderful person in our lives is Mr. Bingley," she said.

Mr. Bingley turned his head at the sound of his name and Elizabeth shook hers. Acknowledgment was all that was needed to encourage her mother's rambling.

"I beg your pardon, Mrs. Bennet?" Bingley asked.

"I said, you are the most wonderful of men, Mr. Bingley," Elizabeth's mother said. "Why, to be so steadfast as to return for our Jane after all this time. You must have such a warm heart, such devotion."

Mr. Bingley shot a look at Jane, clearly embarrassed. "Ah, thank you, Mrs. Bennet."

"What other man would have returned? Who would have been so very brave as to admit he'd been wrong to leave the first time and come back? Such a fine gentleman you are, Mr. Bingley."

"Mama," Elizabeth and Jane said in unison. Elizabeth cast her father a beseeching glance, but she could tell by the amusement on his face that he was enjoying the scene too much to put a stop to it.

"And I must apologize to you, Mr. Bingley, for some of the things I may have inadvertently thought in regards to your suitability and honor," her mother continued. "Why, if I'd but known how steadfast you'd prove, I would have defended you to the grave, even to myself."

Mr. Bingley's face took on a pained expression. "There is no need

196

to apologize, I'm sure."

"I'm so pleased you proved yourself to be the most wonderful of men. When I saw you come rushing over this morning, I knew you'd come to your senses," her mother continued.

Across the table from Elizabeth, Jane looked down at her plate, her cheeks red.

"That's Mr. Bingley, I said to myself," her mother said. "I know why he's here. Such an honest, honorable gentleman has surely realized that he's breaking my poor Jane's heart and he's come to put that right."

"Darcy," Bingley choked out. "It was Darcy. He made me aware that it was time to propose."

Elizabeth turned incredulous eyes on her finance. "Did he?" she asked.

How could he? She'd expressly asked him not to tell Bingley to marry Jane. She didn't want her sister to have a husband who only found her desirable enough at the recommendation of his friend. She'd thought Bingley had proposed out of love, not reason. Whatever would she tell Jane? She couldn't let her marry him. Being wedded to a man who didn't love her would break her gentle heart.

"Mr. Darcy!" her mother cried. "I should have known we had you to thank for this. Oh, what a fine example of a man you are. I knew it from the start, of course. No one can say I didn't."

Darcy looked to her hopefully, but Elizabeth was in no mood to save him. She was so livid over him getting Bingley to propose where there was no firm resolve to, she didn't even want to look at him.

"Mr. Darcy, you are so nice to my daughters," her mother gushed. "You are responsible for the marriages of four of them and now Mary may be able to save enough for a nice dowry. How can I ever thank you?"

Darcy's look became more pleading and Elizabeth stood. She may not want to help him, but she was too angry with him not to be allowed to speak. "Mr. Darcy, I'm sure you would like to see the painting in the hall."

"Certainly," he said, rising as well. "If you'll excuse me, please?" he said to the table at large.

"But, Elizabeth, we're still dining. Can't it wait?" her mother said.

"Mr. Darcy is so found of hunting, Mama, and soon there will be so little light in the hall. I think it must be now."

"Well, off with you then," her mother said. "Don't be too long. You won't want to keep Mr. Darcy from his port. Your father has a fine bottle open to celebrate Jane's engagement."

"Yes, Mama," Elizabeth said, her anger increasing. What had Darcy done? Jane would have to marry Mr. Bingley now, she realized. Jane would wed, and Elizabeth would spend a lifetime trying to keep it from her that her husband didn't love her as much as she loved him. She turned and stomped from the room.

Elizabeth could hear Mr. Darcy following her, but she didn't slow. She didn't stop in the hall beside the ridiculous bird painting, but went straight out the front door into the fading daylight. She wasn't sure she would be able to keep her voice low enough for speaking in the hall. Not with the conversation she planned to have.

"Elizabeth?" Darcy asked, coming up alongside her.

She lengthened her stride, aware that her breath was ragged. She didn't know which was worse, the pain she felt for her sister, her anger, or her utter disappointment in Darcy, the man she'd agreed to spend the remainder of her life with.

"Elizabeth." Darcy grasped her arm, halting her. "You're angry?"

He sounded confused. Of course he did. He wouldn't see that he'd done anything wrong. He was Mr. Darcy and infallible. How had she been fooled into thinking he'd changed from their first meeting?

She pulled her arm away, wrapping both around herself. Turning toward the glory of the sunset, she closed her eyes. She couldn't look on such beauty with so much anger.

Darcy moved to stand at her shoulder. "Why are you angry with me?" he asked.

"You truly don't know?"

"I have no notion at all."

She sighed, opening her eyes. A glance over her shoulder showed him quite close. She looked away, back toward the setting sun. "You made Bingley propose to Jane. I agreed with you. I came around to your thinking and said you were right all along not to tell him to wed her and specifically requested you not do so, and you went and did it, just as you pleased."

"You think that I persuaded Bingley to propose to your sister and that now she will marry a man who doesn't love her?"

She nodded, willing herself not to cry. Poor Jane.

"Then I am angry with you as well," he said.

Elizabeth swung around to face him, dropping her arms to her sides. "What?"

"Or perhaps I mean hurt?" he asked, frowning slightly.

"You are angry with me? Why? Did you expect I should swoon with gratitude for your highhandedness?"

"No."

She narrowed her eyes. Was he trying not to smile? The man was insufferable. "Why then?"

"Because you have so very little faith in me, Elizabeth."

"So little . . ." She shook her head. "You mean for me to believe that you didn't tell Bingley to wed Jane? But he said as much, only moments ago."

"I believe he said that I made him aware that it was time for him to propose."

"I fail to see the difference," she said stiffly.

"I did not suggest Bingley wed your sister," Darcy said firmly. "At breakfast, I expounded on my plans for Jane."

"Your plans?" Was he trying to be confusing? No, there was a glint of amusement lurking in his eyes. He was pleased with himself.

"Well, perhaps I mean our plans," he said, looking down at her. "How we would have your sister come live with us, where we would invite over suitable suitors. Likewise, we would take her to London for the season, a place where her beauty and poise would be sure to attract notice."

"You told Bingley that? At breakfast?" She'd no idea Darcy could be so cunning.

"I expounded on it at moderate length before he grew so incensed he couldn't help but stop me."

"Why, Mr. Darcy, you're devious," Elizabeth said, truly startled.

"So, you see, I did not tell Bingley to marry your sister. I merely suggested that we find someone who was willing to."

Elizabeth felt her face heat. She'd been completely foolish. She groaned, covering her face with her hands. She's jumped straight to the worst possible interpretation of Mr. Bingley's words and maligned Mr. Darcy unpardonably. "I'm sorry," she whispered.

"I daresay you should be," he said.

His smug tone was too much. She dropped her hands to glare at him, only to find him smiling down at her. "You're insufferable," she said.

"Insufferably lovable?" he asked. His eyes took on that intent look, stealing her breath away. "You care so much about your sister marrying for love. It is my hope you also pursue that dream for yourself, because I love you, Elizabeth."

A thrill went through her at his words. She opened her mouth to reply in kind, but then snapped it closed again.

"Elizabeth?" he prompted, his tone touched with worry.

"You signed your letter with Fitzwilliam, but your cousins call you Darcy," she blurted. "No one ever calls you anything but Darcy. How can I tell you how much I love you when I don't know what you want to be called?"

"Then you do love me?" He grinned.

Elizabeth had never seen more than a smile curve Darcy's lips before, and now he was grinning at her. He dropped his head, obviously intent on kissing her.

"I do. I love you, Fitzwilliam Darcy, now and always." She closed her

200

eyes, the lingering rays of sunlight warm on her cheek, and leaned into his kiss.

~ The End ~

About the Authors

Renata McMann

Renata McMann is the pen name of someone who likes to rewrite public domain works. She is fond of thinking "What if?" To learn more about Renata's work and collaborations, visit www.renatamcmann.com.

Summer Hanford

Summer Hanford is primarily a fantasy author, although she enjoys turning her pen to science fiction, Regency and adventure as well. In 2014, Hanford was given the opportunity to team up with McMann and contribute to Renata's passion for *Pride and Prejudice* fan fiction, and is loving every moment of it. To learn more about Summer's other work, visit www.summerhanford.com.

Made in the USA
Columbia, SC
22 November 2019